“You Offere[illegible] Out Of Some S[illegible]

“I owe you my life, Abby Gentry,” said Gray. “I would do much more than that to honor that debt.”

He dragged her into his arms, wrapping her in his embrace. “We’ll make the next couple of months go by quickly and easily, Abby. Have no fear.”

When she raised her head, dark passion flashed in her blazing green eyes. But she made no move to be free of his arms.

“I guess I should thank you for stepping in to help,” she said hoarsely.

She let her hands roam over his powerful chest and felt his skin ripple lightly in response. How wonderful it was to feel what she could do to a man’s body….

Dear Reader,

Top off your summer reading list with six brand-new steamy romances from Silhouette Desire!

Reader favorite Ann Major brings the glamorous LONE STAR COUNTRY CLUB miniseries into Desire with *Shameless* (#1513). This rancher's reunion romance is the first of three titles set in Mission Creek, Texas—where society reigns supreme and appearances are everything. Next, our exciting yearlong series DYNASTIES: THE BARONES continues with *Beauty & the Blue Angel* (#1514) by Maureen Child, in which a dashing naval hero goes overboard for a struggling mom-to-be.

Princess in His Bed (#1515) by *USA TODAY* bestselling author Leanne Banks is the third Desire title in her popular miniseries THE ROYAL DUMONTS. Enjoy the fun as a tough Wyoming rancher loses his heart to a spirited royal-in-disguise. Next, a brooding horseman shows a beautiful rancher the ropes…of desire in *The Gentrys: Abby* (#1516) by Linda Conrad.

In the latest BABY BANK title, *Marooned with a Millionaire* (#1517) by Kristi Gold, passion ignites between a powerful hotel magnate and the pregnant balloonist stranded on his yacht. And a millionaire M.D. brings out the temptress in his tough-girl bodyguard in *Sleeping with the Playboy* (#1518) by veteran Harlequin Historicals and debut Desire author Julianne MacLean.

Get your summer off to a sizzling start with six new passionate, powerful and provocative love stories from Silhouette Desire.

Enjoy!

Melissa Jeglinski
Senior Editor, Silhouette Desire

Please address questions and book requests to:
Silhouette Reader Service
U.S.: 3010 Walden Ave., P.O. Box 1325, Buffalo, NY 14269
Canadian: P.O. Box 609, Fort Erie, Ont. L2A 5X3

The Gentrys: Abby

LINDA CONRAD

Silhouette®
Desire®
Published by Silhouette Books
America's Publisher of Contemporary Romance

SILHOUETTE BOOKS

ISBN 0-373-76516-9

THE GENTRYS: ABBY

This edition published by arrangement with Harlequin Books S.A.

Visit Silhouette at www.eHarlequin.com

Printed in U.S.A.

Books by Linda Conrad

Silhouette Desire

The Cowboy's Baby Surprise #1446
Desperado Dad #1458
Secrets, Lies...and Passion #1470
**The Gentrys: Cinco* #1508
**The Gentrys: Abby* #1516

*The Gentrys

LINDA CONRAD

Born in Brazil to a commercial pilot and his wife, Linda Conrad was raised in south Florida and has been a dreamer and storyteller for as long as she can remember. After her mother's death a few years ago, she moved from her then-home in Texas to Southern California and gave up her previous life as a stockbroker to rededicate herself to her first love: writing.

Linda and her husband, along with a Siamese-mix cat named Sam, recently moved back to south Florida. She's been writing contemporary romances for about five years and loves sharing them with readers. She enjoys growing roses, reading cozy mysteries and sexy romances, and driving her little convertible in the sunshine. But most important, Linda loves learning about—and living with—passion.

It makes Linda's day to hear from readers. Visit with her at www.LindaConrad.com.

To Susan Litman, the best editor ever.
Thanks for letting me push the limits.

Society Bulletin

Mr. & Mrs. T. A. Gentry, V,
To Throw Texas-Size Bash

Local ranchers and newlyweds Cinco and Meredith Gentry are hosting an old-fashioned down-home barbecue on the sixteenth of this month to celebrate the twenty-fourth birthday of Mr. Gentry's sister, Abigail Josephine Gentry.

Abby Jo, as she's known to her friends, recently returned to Gentry Wells after earning her degree in Ranch Management at Texas A&M.

The birthday barbecue is expected to be the social occasion of the season. The lucky party-goers will not only enjoy Texas-size portions of food and drink, but can expect a good ol' Texas-size heap of fun and dancing till dawn. Rumor even has it that one of Texas's favorite country-western bands, the Dixie Dudes, will be playing for guests' enjoyment.

This writer, for one, will be polishing her silver buckles and trying on her new snakeskin dancing boots in anticipation of a good-time Texas shindig.

One

Abby Gentry winced as she climbed down from her saddle onto the scrub-filled, back-country dirt of Gentry Ranch. She grounded her horse under a mesquite tree, pulled her heavy rope from its ring and glanced over toward the dry-wash. Every bone and muscle in her body ached.

She was young enough that riding out here on the range for the past ten or twelve hours should've been no big deal. In one week she would be just twenty-four, and her body ought to be able to withstand a lot more punishment than that. Heck, she was raised on the back of a horse. Sighing, she chalked the aches and pains up to sitting on her back end for too long while away at college.

She pulled off her bandanna, pushed back the black felt Resistol, and wiped the sweat from her forehead and the back of her neck before plopping the hat back onto her head. Stomping around in her dusty riding boots, she kicked the kinks out of her legs. Abby had always thought that ranching chores were the most important part of life on the range, and these days she needed to be sure to take a more visible role in them. Her dream of becoming the Gentry Ranch foreman seemed to be almost within her reach.

Abby twisted around to see if her trail partner, Billy Bob Jackson, had ridden into view. She didn't see any sign of the cranky old man she'd known for most of her life. He'd told her to go on ahead when he needed a little break.

The plan was for her to ride along the fence line at a slow pace until he caught up. But as she'd guided her horse along the rim of this deep dry-wash, she'd spotted the dark shadow of a downed critter at the bottom.

She figured the animal was another one of the dead or dying yearlings they'd been coming across as they checked the fences and windmills in this section of the ranch over the past three days. For several months now the Gentry Ranch had been losing calves to some kind of predator. Part of her job out here was to save the animals that could be saved and to find evidence of what had killed the others.

If the critter in this wash was already gone and she couldn't help him, Abby at least hoped to make an educated guess as to what had killed him. She anchored her rope to the mesquite and, at the rim of the dry wash, she circled the free end of the rope and stepped into it, tightening the loop under her arms.

Actually, she was relieved not to have to explain anything to Billy Bob before climbing down the jagged rocks lining the ravine. He would've wanted to be the one to go over the side and check out the carcass.

While she slowly lowered herself over the rim, the blazing afternoon sun made waves of heat reflect off the white limestone boulders lying at the bottom of the wash. Abby felt the very blood in her veins begin to boil as she struggled to reach the floor of the wash fifteen feet below.

When her boots hit the ground, she slipped on the loose gravel but quickly recovered. She dragged the rope up and over her head, freeing herself to turn and scramble back to the dark, still form lying in the shadow of a boulder a few feet away.

Nearing the shadow, she saw the truth. She hissed a breath through her teeth when she realized this was no animal…but a man. A terribly injured and possibly dead man who hadn't moved or moaned the whole time she'd been climbing down the rock ravine.

Abby squeezed past a couple of boulders and had just enough room to kneel beside him. She knew then why she'd thought this was some kind of animal. Everything about him exuded darkness and shadow: black hair, deeply bronzed skin, and he'd dressed in black jeans with an inky-colored, long-sleeved shirt.

It hit her almost immediately that this man must be Native American, which seemed highly unusual for Castillo County. In fact, she could only think of one American Indian that she'd ever seen in these parts. Surely, this man couldn't be the same boy who'd taken her side against a bully in high school ten years ago. She'd dreamed about him occasionally since then, and maybe her imagination had taken over her good sense.

Abby put aside the old dreams and the decidedly sexual images she'd kept in her heart for so long and forced herself to concentrate on saving the injured man. Could he be saved?

The little gash on his temple and the small trickle of blood that had dried against his cheek shouldn't have caused him to be unconscious, she thought. He might have blacked out for a moment from such a head trauma, but to be so still for so long…

Perhaps he'd fallen into the wash from above. She glanced up at the rim and shook her head. Well, if he had, he'd probably broken his neck.

She checked for a pulse. He was alive! His heart rate was faint, and as she listened carefully, she heard him wheezing when he tried to breathe. But he was most assuredly alive.

All her first-aid and emergency medical training nagged at her good sense and reminded her not to move him. No telling what injuries he had. Still, she was all the help he was likely to get. If he was going to make it out of this dry wash alive, she was his only hope.

Abby propped open his mouth, trying to find any obstructions that might be causing those gurgling sounds. When her hand touched his chin, she nearly pulled it back with a jerk. His skin was so hot, her first thought was that she'd been burned. A fleeting image of smooth fire flashed in her head, but she forced herself to stay focused on keeping him alive.

Not much blood and no other obvious wounds. What had befallen this man?

When she reached to open the top button on his shirt to give him a little more air, Abby took a good look at his beautiful face. Even in his unconscious state she could see the pain written in his expression. But she also saw the dark and noble features she'd remembered all these years, older now but somehow even more compelling. Oh my God. This man really was the boy hero of her dreams.

Trying her best to remain professional, she opened his shirt collar and immediately saw the telltale swelling at his neck. Uh-oh. She had a feeling she knew what had happened.

Quickly, Abby checked his arms but didn't find what she was looking for. Her gaze quickly took in his long torso and grazed down his legs, halting when she saw that his left thigh was swollen and straining the stitching of his jeans. Exactly what she'd feared. Snakebite.

Removing her knife from its sheath on her belt, she began slicing his pants leg. The material was so tough she had to rip and tear at it. At one point she even had to use her teeth, hands and the knife.

Finally the chore was done, and she frantically searched his skin for the two telltale holes. By now his lower thigh was twice its size, bruised green, purple and yellow. Turning him on his side, she found the wounds on the back of his leg just above his knee. Looked as if a large rattler had done this job.

She eased him all the way over and carefully arranged his head so that his breathing was a little quieter. As she did, the images of broad shoulders and rippled muscles blasted her with memories and tender feelings. But there wasn't enough time for her to be gentle, let alone pay attention to much else. He might be running out of time.

Abby left him for a few moments to dash back to her rope, still dangling over the side of the ravine. She climbed back up to the top of the ravine and found Billy Bob waiting there for her return.

"What's going on down there?" he asked as she headed for her canteen and snakebite kit. "You fixin' to nurse a steer? You'd be better off using your rifle to take him out of his misery, missy."

"No, it's not one of the yearlings," she gasped

through the fear that made her voice raspy. "It's a man. And he's hurt bad."

Abby gulped down a near-hysterical sob. She'd never helped anyone this gravely ill before. If he died…

Back at the bottom of the wash, she thanked heaven for the rattlesnake antivenom. Abby did exactly as she'd been trained. First she'd used the Sawyer Pump extractor to draw out as much surface venom as possible. Next she'd injected the antivenom.

The rest would be up to God.

Within a few minutes she could see the swelling begin to subside. He'd started to breath easier and his eyelids fluttered as he seemed to fight for consciousness.

Perhaps he was in shock. She poured canteen water on her red bandanna and wiped his forehead, eventually leaving the wet cloth lightly covering his face to keep the sun off. Abby knew she had to get him to the hospital. He needed professional medical attention.

The cell phones were worthless out here, and they would need to ride for hours to find help. But first he had to be moved out of this harsh sun. How on earth would she manage that?

She screwed up her mouth and looked around at the walls of the wash. Well, there was nothing to do but try the best she could. A man's life hung on her efforts.

Fortunately, Billy Bob had known what to do. He had rigged up a makeshift stretcher, made from a few sturdy mesquite branches, some rope and a couple of vines that grew alongside the rim of the wash. In the meantime, she'd used the elastic bandage from the first-aid kit to keep pressure on the wound.

After a couple of trips up and down the walls of the ravine, she and Billy Bob used their ropes and horses to pull the stretcher up past the sharp rocks along the sides of the dry wash. She was breathing hard and nearly ready to pass out by the time she'd finished guiding the man's inert form as he lay tied firmly between the branches. Her long-sleeved denim shirt was soaked through, and the sweat poured from every inch of her body.

Billy Bob handed his trail canteen over to her.

Abby put a few drops of water on the unconscious man's cracked lips and took a couple of swallows of the metallic-tasting water herself. Then Billy Bob did the same.

Abby finished packing her saddlebags. ''We'd better figure a way to get him out of the sun,'' she told Billy Bob. ''Line shack twenty-three isn't far away, is it?''

'''Bout a half mile back up the fence line,'' Billy Bob answered over his shoulder. He was rigging up the stretcher behind her horse, Patsy, in the old Indian-squaw style.

''Good thing, too,'' he said. ''Don't rightly think those branches will hold together for much farther than that.''

Abby agreed wholeheartedly. Their lashing ability left a lot to be desired. But the makeshift rig should remain in one piece just long enough. She hoped.

The line shack turned out to be only a quarter mile away, but it took them much longer than she'd thought to reach it. By the time she dismounted and opened up the shack, the harsh, late-spring sun hung low in the sky, casting long shadows from every tree and rock. The stretcher, which had surprisingly held together until now, began to unravel and would soon be in tatters.

The heat in the little cabin was intense. She quickly threw open the front door and all the windows except the one that had been broken and boarded up. A dry, dusty breeze finally blew through the one room and dropped the temperature, but not nearly enough to make it comfortable.

While Billy Bob struggled to untie the stretcher from Patsy, Abby unpacked the blanket rolls that served as bedding for the cabin's one cot and one bunk. Then, despite the extreme temperature in the cabin, she started a fire in the cookstove. She wanted to heat some water so she could clean the man's wounds first thing.

''Well, ain't that a kick in the britches.'' Billy Bob elbowed open the door that had blown shut in the hot breeze. He half carried, half dragged the injured man inside and lowered him onto the cot.

It was the first time that Billy Bob had stopped long enough to get a good look at the man he'd helped save. The sight of an American Indian in this part of Texas was pretty rare these days. Rarer still to see one on Gentry Ranch land. Billy Bob just stood and stared down at him.

The injured man groaned once and opened his eyes, trying to come out of his groggy fog. Abby got only a momentary glance at the deep, black eyes. But that was enough.

For sure, it was her high school heartthrob. She'd all but forgotten.

No, that wasn't quite right. She'd never forgotten those mesmerizing eyes. Put them out of her mind maybe. Buried the uneasy sensual feelings way down, deep enough not to be consciously remembered. But never totally forgotten.

''That there's the Injun who lives on the Skaggs Ranch, ain't it?'' Billy Bob scratched his stubbled chin and squinted up his eyes in thought.

Indeed. He most certainly was the ''Injun'' who was the stepson of the man who owned the ranch next door. Abby searched her subconscious for shreds of memories.

''Yep. His name is Gray Wolf Parker and he's Skaggs's stepson. Abby hadn't seen him since she'd been a high school freshman and he was the new senior. But the rest of her memories had to wait for a moment alone.

''Billy Bob, you know the cell phone won't work out here, don't you?'' she asked the old man.

Billy Bob looked her way and nodded.

''You think you can watch Gray while I ride back toward the big house?'' she asked shortly. ''I figure it's only twenty miles or so to where the cell phone will be in range. I'll give the helicopter paramedics aerial directions to the line shack when I can reach them.''

Billy Bob frowned at her, shuffled his feet and tried to knock the accumulated dust off his work hat by slapping it against the side of his even dustier chaps-covered thigh. Maybe she shouldn't have sounded so demanding with her request. After all, her goal was to become his boss soon. She really needed him, as well as the rest of the men, to be on her side and start seeing her as the new foreman.

Billy Bob shook his head. ''Look, missy. You already went down that wash when it was too dangerous. I wasn't there to stop you, but Jake and Cinco would have my hide if I let you go riding off across the ranch alone in the dark of night. Cinco gave me strict orders to keep you safe.'' Before she could make any reply, he'd stepped outside the door, and she heard him spitting out the chewing tobacco.

Dang. Several thoughts flashed through her head at once. In the first place, he'd called her missy again. She hated that little-girl term. When would she ever make it to just plain ol' Abby? Even the old-lady term ''ma'am'' would sit easier with her.

And secondly, why had her brother been talking to the men about her safety? He had no right to meddle in her business.

''I'll ride back toward the ranch,'' Billy Bob mumbled when he reentered the room. ''I know this part of the ranch better 'n you. The man's out cold and you're a better nurse 'n me, anyhow. You stay here with him.''

Fighting with all kinds of emotions, she hesitated. She wanted to be the decision maker now. But it was too soon to force the issue. Yes, she was a Gentry. And yes, technically she owned a third of the ranch. But she still hadn't proven she was worthy of the respect it would take to make the hands, young and old alike, follow her lead.

She swallowed her pride and realized Billy Bob was probably right. He did know this part of the ranch better than she did. He had the best chance of getting within phone range in the fastest time. He was the logical choice to go.

But she surely didn't want to be the one stuck here alone with the sexy and potent Gray Parker.

Whew! Where did that silliness come from? Her injured neighbor was probably in shock and should remain out cold for most of the night. She really had nothing to fear except her own uncalled-for lusting. Besides, he needed her to finish the job she'd started and see to it that he got home alive.

Handing Billy Bob the phone, she gave him instructions and kept reminding herself she had nothing to worry about.

Billy Bob mounted his mare and stared down at her.

"You done a right fair job of saving Parker's life today. Your father would've been mighty proud of you, Abby Jo. But I'm reserving judgment on whether you'll survive as foreman when the time comes."

It was the longest speech she'd ever heard from the man.

Billy Bob nudged his horse, turning to head up the fence line toward home. "Take care of yourself and the young buck. The chopper'll be here by dawn." He tipped his hat toward her. "You have my word, ma'am."

Ma'am? He'd actually called her ma'am. Well, that was at least a beginning.

When Abby returned to the cabin, she discovered the cool shadows of nightfall had finally reached them, relieving the oppressive heat. It was already so dark that she had to light a couple of kerosene lanterns.

The water pot she'd set on the stove had begun to boil, so she started getting down to work. She put a little of the hot water in the sink and washed her hands and face. It felt so good to scrape off the trail dust and sweat that she nearly cried. Next, she wanted to clean up her patient and make him more comfortable.

Patient. Now wouldn't *that* be an excellent way for her to treat him—as well as to think of him?

Abby stepped to his side and looked down. Uh-oh. She suddenly realized she'd actually have to look at him—touch him—in order to treat him. The teenage crush, the nervous shyness whenever he'd been around, all of that came back to irritate her now.

She stood still as a fence post, studying Gray's body. He'd obviously changed some since she'd last seen him.

Funny, they lived on adjoining ranches but she hadn't laid eyes on him in almost ten years.

The last time she'd seen him, he'd been a boy of eighteen with a tight, lanky build and an even tighter expression perpetually plastered on his face. Now he was truly an adult male. Still firm and athletic, his shoulders had broadened and his body had filled out. Whew, baby. She closed her eyes and counted to ten, trying to stem a zinging shock of nerves that she couldn't quite name.

When she opened her eyes, she noticed his straight black hair was much shorter than she'd remembered. Thick and full, it didn't even touch his neck in back.

In high school, his hair had been long and flowing, although he normally tied it back with a rawhide thong. For a young girl that hair had not only been a curiosity but also a terrifically erotic draw.

Now the short, thick strands seemed to be begging for her touch. Her hand reached out, of its own accord, but she dragged it back and vowed to concentrate on his wounds.

The memories still came to haunt her. Gray hadn't been particularly friendly with the rest of the kids at school. He'd stood aside and watched them with those dangerous, ebony eyes. But that didn't stop most of the girls from drooling over him—Abby included.

But the eyes had stopped her. They scared her. There was just something in them that she couldn't understand. Something that made her uncomfortable—jumpy and nervous.

Besides, Abby didn't go gaga for boys. She didn't want to date them. If they could be buddies, fine. Otherwise, she could outride, outwrangle and outwork any of them. And to this day, she liked it just that way.

Nevertheless, she did remember Gray taking her side

once and being her real-life hero. She found herself swallowing the lump that had formed in her throat by just looking at him. His eyes weren't staring at her now. They were closed, but she could see the pain etched across his features just the same. She reached for his shirt buttons and decided she'd put these idiotic feelings aside and take care of the injured man.

Determined and dedicated, she managed not to think as she unbuttoned his shirt and rolled him out of it.

There. See? It was easy to—

Whoa! She found herself frozen in place and staring at his chest. It was broad, rippled and so manly it nearly knocked the breath from her lungs. In the shimmering lamplight, she could see the sheen of sweat spreading over his smooth, hairless skin and shining like a glittering lake in the moonlight.

She couldn't help it when her gaze dropped lower, heading for his waist—and lower yet—to the part of him covered by tight, worn jeans, and shouting to her that he was uniquely male. And more so than most, she'd noted.

But her gaze suddenly returned to a patch of scars, spreading out across his abdomen like the wings of a bird. Gray had been cut. But they weren't recent wounds, and they really did have some pattern to them.

The urge to follow the featherlike scars with her fingertips nearly consumed her. She longed to soothe his jagged skin—to heal his old, echoing pains.

Abby pulled her hand back before she actually touched him, and shook her shoulders, trying to keep focused. He needed her help to live. She could do this. He was groggy and seemed to be going in and out of a semiconscious state. At times he could almost focus his gaze on her, at others his eyes were closed. She prayed that most times he'd keep those dark eyes shut.

A half hour later, as she put the soapy water and wet towels away, she congratulated herself on remaining so calm and detached. She'd known that her practical nature would win out. After all, he was just a man. Normally, she had no trouble ignoring any minor tingles when she looked at a well-built specimen of manhood. Especially an injured one.

Fixing for a little hot chicken broth for the two of them, she reflected on her actions today and felt good about them. She'd been strong, levelheaded and decisive. Exactly the qualities that her ranch management professor at college had said would be required of a professional foreman.

Being the foreman on the Gentry Ranch was all she'd ever dreamed about doing with her life.

After a while Gray became coherent enough for her to hold his head up and spoon a bit of broth into his mouth. As she did, she thought about how proud of her Jake would be.

He'd been the ranch foreman for as long as she could remember. Always her idol and role model, Jake Gomez had encouraged her to go for her dreams and try for his job when the time came.

Of course, convincing her older brother, Cinco, to give her the job was going to take every bit of strength and determination she could muster.

Abby set aside the bowl of broth, relieved to see that Gray's features looked decidedly calmer. He didn't seem to be in as much pain. Maybe he'd sleep through the night.

After she'd washed the bowls and spoons, she figured that if he could rest, perhaps she could catch a couple of winks, as well. She wouldn't really sleep soundly, she needed to be alert to any changes in Gray's breathing. But a cat nap or two couldn't hurt anything.

Abby got comfortable by opening a few buttons on her shirt and loosening her heavy work belt. Then she shut off two of the lanterns and turned down the light on the one she'd kept next to Gray's cot. The lamplight flickered against the ceiling of the cabin, sending eerie shadows to play hide-and-seek with her mind.

Abby shivered in the heat, but decided she was being silly again. Heading toward the bunk, she smelled smoke. But she'd put out the stove's fire ages ago after heating the broth. And the lanterns only smelled like kerosene, not smoke.

Smiling at her own foolishness, she moved to the windows and made sure they were wide open. It hadn't cooled down much at all since the sun had set, but it was certainly more comfortable than when the sun was high in the sky.

At the window she took a deep breath, intending to clear her head. But the smell of smoke was even stronger outside. Now she realized not only was she definitely smelling smoke, but pipe-tobacco smoke at that.

But where…who…would be smoking? The first real sense of panic grabbed at her gut, sending adrenaline shooting through her veins.

Quickly she barred the windows and barricaded the door, listening all the while for a sound from Patsy that might mean another horse or some intruder was nearby. But the complete silence of the darkness worried her even more than those sounds might have. Where were the night sounds? The usual whispers of tree frogs and crickets and the soft spring breeze through the leaves? All those normal noises were strangely quiet.

Abby picked up her rifle from its place in the corner

and sat down in the chair she'd dragged over beside Gray's cot. She wrapped her arms around her body, as if doing so would hold the world together, no matter what.

The silence was deafening. And the smell of tobacco smoke was stronger than ever.

Instinctively, she set the rifle down beside her and reached a hand to place against Gray's forehead, to satisfy herself that he was still breathing. He seemed peaceful enough, and his skin was cool and dry. But just then, a low drumming beat suddenly began pulsing through the night.

Drums? The distant sounds set fire to her blood. Soon the vibrations rang inside her body. The pounding snaked through her, almost as if a living, breathing creature inhabited her arteries, taking over the beating of her heart.

She closed her eyes and held on tightly to her sanity. Another sound, the magic sound of an ancient flute, drifted through the walls, haunting her unconscious mind.

Keeping her eyelids shut against whatever evil might befall them, she reached out toward Gray. She needed the touch of another human being.

When her hand touched only emptiness, her eyes popped open. Right before she fainted in a heap on the hardwood floor, Abby's brain refused to believe what her sight had clearly revealed.

The cot stood cold and empty. Gray was gone.

Two

"Come with me, Gray, my son."

"Father? *Ahpi?*" The very strong sensation of fingers gripping his forearm confused Gray. Was this really his father beckoning him to follow? Impossible. His father had died years ago. Did that mean Gray had somehow also died from the poisonous snakebite? Had his brother the rattlesnake sent him into the land of his ancestors?

Gray didn't want to die. Intrigued by the memory of the girl who'd fought to save him, he wanted more time. He remembered her heroic efforts, even though he hadn't been able to talk to her or help himself. The echoing feel of her cool hands on his feverish body continued to calm his spirit.

Gray looked around but saw only dark images, swirling clouds of ghostlike shadows. "Father, where do you take me?" He heard the shrill call of the red-tailed hawk and beyond that, the ever-present drumbeat of his own heart.

"*Nemene,* our people, wish to speak to you through the misty shrouds of time. You will listen with your heart."

"Yes, *Ahpi.* As you wish, but..."

Before Gray could finish his sentence, he noticed the image of his own mother, standing next to him. The sharp pain of grief was the first arrow to enter his heart.

"Mother."

"No, my son. I am *Pia,* the mother of all the people, come to you in an image that will imprint itself on your soul. Banish the pain of your grief, Gray Wolf Parker. Your mother wishes it. Open yourself to the wisdom of the ancient spirits."

Gray shook his head. This had to be some kind of weird dream or hallucination brought on by the snake-bite. Or...maybe he really was dead.

"No, son." The old woman answered his query without him having to give voice to it. "Your body has not left our earth home. We've come to give you *puha*...great medicine. We've come to give you your vision."

"But why? Why me?"

Gray could feel the smiles of many, even though suddenly his mother's image had disappeared and he could see no one through the wispy mists.

"You are one of the people. That is enough," the shadowed figure said. "You work to bring the herd back to the land of the ancient hunters. The council honors you as chief...as you honor us in deed."

Another voice spoke without being seen. "You will live to finish your quest. You will have a long and fruitful life, give many braves to the *nemene.* Your vision has been decided."

Gray was confused. He still couldn't understand what they were trying to tell him. "But, father. I don't..."

"Remember that a chief of the people provides protection and loyalty. Honor, my son, above all things will provide great medicine and long life to you."

The voices and the low drumbeat began to fade. Once again Gray felt the pain. Funny. He hadn't noticed the throbbing ache in his leg until now.

His ancestors had one more whispered thing to say. "Honor, Gray Wolf Parker. Do not forget. Honor always the one that has been chosen."

And then they were gone.

Gray took a deep breath and realized his eyes were closed. When he opened them, it took a few minutes of struggling to focus on his surroundings.

The dim light from the lantern illuminated the tiny cabin where he found himself lying on a low cot. He tried to make out the forms and furniture, whirling in the flickering shadows from the lamp. But his head swam and his heart raced.

He slowly swung his legs over the side of the cot and felt the burning sting in his thigh. Gritting his teeth, he put his feet flat on the floor and sat up.

When he was sitting upright on the cot, he took a short inventory of himself and the place. He noted that his shirt was gone, his pants leg had been removed and someone had put an elastic bandage tightly around his wounded thigh.

The girl? he remembered. His eyes became accustomed to the darkness, and he checked his surroundings to see if someone else might be nearby. And that's when he saw her.

He'd practically stepped on her as he moved his feet to sit up. Sprawled out on the floor below him, she appeared to have passed out. With a sudden spit of panic, Gray reached down to touch her cheek. Warm, satiny and very much alive. He breathed a low sigh of relief.

He smiled at her relaxed form. Through the haze of pain and delirium of the past twenty-four hours, he remembered her fighting strength and the gentleness she'd used to help him. Gazing at her now, he noticed she looked much smaller and finer boned than he'd imagined at first.

Her hair shone with red highlights in the lamplight, and he could see the freckles streaking across her nose. She appeared to be more of a child than seemed possible, given all that she'd accomplished to save him.

What was she doing sleeping on the floor?

Gray reached for her. "Uh. Excuse me. Are you comfortable down there?" He shook her shoulder with as gentle a touch as he could manage.

"Wha...?" She pulled away from him and sat up.

Her hair spilled over her eyes. She brushed it back with her fingers and blew the rest of the strands out of her face.

"You're here! And you're—" she took a deep breath "—alive?"

"Yes, of course, thanks to you. I remember you saving my life, don't I?"

Her eyes widened, and she seemed struck dumb. In the deep shadows of lamplight, he couldn't quite tell what color they were but they looked like they might be green. Green eyes had always fascinated him.

"I only did what anyone would've. But I thought..."

She squeezed her eyes tight, and when she opened them again they fixated on his face. ''Do you mind if I touch you?''

The question sent a chill running down his chest, exploding with a surprisingly intense heat deep in his gut.

''What's the matter?'' he ventured, as he took her hand. ''You look pale. Are you ill?''

She placed her free hand against her forehead. ''No. But when I smelled the smoke and heard the drums...and then...you were gone.'' With the help of his extended hand, she got to her feet, standing over him as he sat on the edge of the cot. ''Only I guess that's impossible, isn't it? I must've been dreaming.''

Drums? ''Tell me about the drums,'' he demanded in a hoarse whisper. ''Did they seem to come from everywhere at once? Did you feel them seeping inside you like they belonged to the air and the wind?''

She nodded sharply, then stared at him. ''Do you know what they were? Did you hear them, too?''

He sat forward and leaned his forehead into his palms. Man, his head hurt.

''I thought *I* must've been dreaming,'' he groaned.

''Tell me about it.''

''I have to think.'' He rubbed his temples. ''I can't think.''

She placed a hand on his shoulder. ''It's all right, Gray. We can talk about it later. You've been through a lot.''

His chin jerked up. ''You know my name? But I don't know who you are. I remember your help in the dry wash, but I can't remember ever meeting you before.'' The frustration was evident in his dark-rimmed eyes.

Abby swallowed the small ego buster. She clearly remembered the time he'd knocked Bigelow Yates off his horse when that bully had decided to use her as a lassoing post. A few of the dumber adolescent boys had oftentimes made her the brunt of their jokes back then. Probably because she'd fought back and refused to flutter her eyelashes and cry like the other girls.

But although Gray had been her hero that day and had always treated her with respect, there was no reason on earth why he should remember. It was a long time ago, and they'd both changed over the years.

"I'm Abby Gentry. We're neighbors. And...we went to high school together for a year."

"Abby Gentry?" He shook his head and wiped a palm over his mouth. "As in *the* Gentrys? I can't..." He rubbed at his temples again.

"Don't...don't try. I doubt if I was very memorable." She sympathetically placed her hand on his shoulder but quickly withdrew it when the feel of his bare skin sent a shock down her arm. "Let's, uh, try something easier. What were you doing in that dry wash without a horse? And how on earth did you let that rattler get the best of you? Don't you know better than to turn your back on a snake?"

He grimaced and rubbed his hand across his mouth again. "Can I have a little water?"

Abby was startled. How cruel could she be? Here the poor man had been near death and fighting for his life until just a little while ago, and instead of treating him like a patient she was interrogating him.

When she looked a little closer, she saw the dark, purplish circles under his eyes. "Sure. I'm sorry. Don't talk. Rest. The paramedic helicopter should be here soon." She quickly got him a cup of the bottled water.

He took a sip, cleared his throat and handed the cup back to her. "I owe you an explanation." His gaze landed on her eyes, and his scrutiny made her nervous again. ''In fact, I owe you much more.... I owe you my life.''

Abby shook her head sharply. ''Really, I was just glad I was trained to help. Don't give it a second thought.''

His lips crooked in a semblance of a smile. ''I will do more than give it a second thought, Abby Gentry. Ask anything of me. My life is yours. Forever.''

Abby backed up a step, trying to put distance between them. She didn't quite know how to take his fierce and serious manner. Shaking her head over and over, she began to deny his words, but he silenced her with a raised hand.

''We will not speak of it now. But I'll honor the debt with every breath.'' He eased back on the cot, staring up at the ceiling with unfocused eyes. ''I do remember that I was checking on the herd. My mustangs have been having some trouble with your fence lines for the past few weeks.

''Then, when I discovered that a section of the Gentry Ranch fence was down near the dry wash, I began to worry that the ponies might've wandered through. I was riding Thunder Cloud...'' He let his words trail off for a second. ''We ride together in the old way. No saddle. No bridle or bit. No horseshoes. Anyway, I thought I heard a horse's whinny coming from the wash. I didn't want to force Thunder Cloud into the rocks, so I dismounted and left him on the rim.''

''You left your horse? I should go back and get him. I'll see to it that he gets fed and watered then returned to your ranch.''

He shot a surprised glance in her direction. ''You're worried about my pony?''

"Of course." She said it so directly, so simply, that Gray was amazed.

A Gentry would be concerned over one horse? And another man's horsc at that?

"Do not trouble yourself over Thunder Cloud," he told her. "He goes where he wishes, and he's more at home on the range than in a corral."

Gray still needed to finish the story, his pride be damned. "As for the snake, I never saw him, never even heard him. I don't understand how I might have disturbed his nap.

"I track with the Comanche wisdom," he continued. "My grandfather taught me. The *nemene* belong to the earth, they do not trample upon it."

She tilted her head, lowered her chin. "Do you remember how you got that wound on your head?"

Gray touched the spot on his temple that now was swollen and bruised. "No. I must have hit my head on a rock after the snake startled me."

Abby nodded. "That would explain why you didn't just walk away from the rattler bite and ride for help."

He couldn't remember. The sounds of the beating drums had been so strong in his head that they obliterated everything else.

Was he going crazy? He needed to call his grandfather to ask about the dream—and why this Gentry girl had heard the drums, too.

At his first thought of the eerie drumbeats, Gray could swear he heard them again. But of course, that was nuts. A minute later he recognized the sounds. A helicopter was landing outside.

"Ah. The paramedics are here," Abby said as she headed to take the barricades from the door. "It must be dawn."

"I'm okay now," Gray muttered. "I remember you administered antivenom. I was very lucky you carry such things on the range."

He didn't need the embarrassment of having to be airlifted off the ranch for a simple snakebite. "I'm well enough to find my own way back to the Skaggs Ranch. Thunder Cloud won't have gone too far."

Abby started toward him and smiled—the first real smile he could remember having graced her face. With the early-morning light seeping through the open door and under the cracks in the window coverings, Gray finally saw what he'd hoped was true. Her eyes were a gray-green.

The swift arrow of lust he felt as he watched her walking to his side left him shaken. There was nothing overtly sexy about this woman, yet…

That must've been it, he mused. For the first time, he'd actually recognized *the woman* inside the tomboy's form.

It had been so long since the spark of desire had shot through him, he barely recognized the feeling. Returning to Texas after his mother's death had only brought him anguish, pain and hard work. Not women.

He didn't have time for that nonsense now, either. Especially since it involved the one who'd saved his life, and most especially because she was one of the rich Gentrys. Besides, as a white woman she did not have the blood of the *nemene* running through her veins.

"You look like you're going to survive, but you haven't even gotten to your feet yet," she said. "Why don't you try standing first? Then you can decide about the paramedics."

Abby took his arm, assisting him to get up. His head

swam and his stomach rolled. Apparently seeing his weakness, she gently pushed him back down on the cot.

"Well, that answers the question. If you can't stand, you can't walk back home."

Gray groaned with misery and embarrassment as two men in jumpsuits, carrying large plastic cases, piled into the little room. "Sorry it took so long, Miss Gentry. We've been filled in on the patient's condition, so we should have him stabilized and delivered to the regional hospital within a few minutes. Don't worry."

The paramedics had been true to their words. Over Gray's protests, they'd taken his vital signs, administered oxygen from a portable bottle and started an IV containing fluids to rehydrate him. Within minutes they had him loaded into the chopper and on his way.

Afterward, as Abby rode alone to the main house, she'd had a long discussion with herself about letting imagination overtake reality. Now, a few hours later, after a bath and nap, Abby began to feel human again.

She must've been exhausted and in a state of shock herself to imagine smoke and drums last night. And to believe that somehow Gray's body had been spirited away.... Well, it was all just a crazy dream.

Abby had more important things to attend to this afternoon. She needed to give her older brother, Cinco, a piece of her mind. How dare he go over her head and speak to Billy Bob and Jake about her safety?

She knew he'd always been wrapped up in security issues, that he'd felt responsible for her and their brother, Cal, ever since their parents' death. But in return, Cinco knew about her dreams of becoming the foreman on Gentry Ranch. She'd told him many times.

To think he'd actually told Billy Bob to watch out for

her. Here she was, trying to prove that she was a capable ranch hand and nearly ready to become the foreman for the entire Gentry spread, and Cinco continued to undercut her efforts. She loved her brother, but he had to start treating her like an adult who could take care of herself.

She stormed through the old homestead, stalking Cinco, but he was nowhere to be found. Abby slapped her thigh with the leather gloves she was about to put on. Dang, but he led a charmed life.

When she pushed into the kitchen through the swinging doors and found her new sister-in-law, Meredith, Abby's mood lightened considerably.

There hadn't been a woman besides herself and Lupe, the old housekeeper, on Gentry Ranch since her mother's disappearance over twelve years ago. Abby had developed a real soft spot for Meredith, a tough ex-Air Force pilot who possessed a sympathetic and warm center. Besides, her sister-in-law could make Cinco listen to reason.

Her brother had generally been an insufferable control freak for the past twelve years. But since getting married, he'd softened some. At least, she'd thought so until Billy Bob's words yesterday on the range.

"Abby Jo! I'm so glad to see you." Meredith quickly embraced her. "When we heard about what happened out on the range, we thought you might've been in trouble...or hurt."

Abby denied her own need for the warmth and comfort of her sister-in-law's hug and stepped away. "Of all the danged silliness. *You* might not know me well enough to be sure I can take care of myself, but Cinco does."

She narrowed her eyes and continued. "Where is the great ranch manager? I have a few things to say to him."

Meredith smiled and held out a plateful of chocolate chip cookies. ''Lupe made these just this morning. Have a couple. They're her usual triumphs.''

It would be impossible to pass up any of Lupe's cookies. Abby took a handful and stuffed one in her mouth.

''I think your brother is still out on the range,'' Meredith said, finally answering her original question. ''He decided to ride up to line shack twenty-three—'' she put the plate back on the counter ''—just in case you might need anything on your way back.''

Abby nearly spit out the mouthful of cookie crumbs. ''What? Why that—''

''Hold on, honey.'' Meredith took hold of her shoulders with a firm grip. ''Don't go crazy over him worrying about you. You've known him all your life. He's a worrier. You know that part of him will never totally change.''

Meredith shrugged and tossed her thick, gold braid over her shoulder. ''I've come to the conclusion that I like having him concerned about *my* welfare. You know that doesn't mean he's trying to control your life. It just means he loves you.''

Abby finally gave in. ''I know he loves me, Meri, and I love him. But I want him to see that I'm grown-up enough to take care of myself and that I know what I want from life.''

Her sister-in-law slowly shook her head. ''Oh, he knows that you've grown up, all right. I'm not supposed to tell you this yet, but he's planning a big shindig for your birthday—inviting all the eligible bachelors in the county, too.''

Once again cookie crumbs went spewing over the kitchen. ''What? But why on earth...''

Meredith slung an arm around her. ''He thinks you

must be lonely way out here. He's concerned that you haven't been seeing friends or dating since you've been home from school."

"Well, if that doesn't beat all." Abby hung her head. "I can't believe he didn't remember that I *never* dated anyone in high school...and I certainly don't need a man messing up my life now. How could he just go off and invite people without speaking to me about it first?"

Meredith took a step back and studied her. "You never dated in high school?"

Abby shook her head.

"How about in college?"

The incredulous tone in Meredith's voice caused Abby some embarrassment, but she didn't have anything to hide. Men just hadn't fitted into her dreams. Lots of women in this modern world lived long and fruitful lives without being tied to a man. She'd always planned to be one of them.

She shook her head and headed for another cookie.

"Are you telling me that you've never 'been' with a man?" Meredith asked in amazement.

"Of course not," Abby managed to say before stuffing her mouth again. "Why would I?"

Meredith chuckled. "Oh, honey, I can see why Cinco worries so much about you."

Abby wrinkled up her face but couldn't protest with her mouth still full.

"Listen up, Abby Jo Gentry." Meredith straightened to her full five foot ten. "You *will* go to this party Cinco's planned. You *will* talk to some of the men. And you *will* enjoy yourself."

Meredith kissed her on the cheek. "That's an order."

Three

A week later Gray climbed the back steps to the kitchen of the Skaggses' main house. His body still ached, but at least he hadn't been forced to stay in the hospital for more than a few hours.

"You must have a strong constitution, son." One of the doctors told him as he signed the papers to send him home. "Most people would've been down for a week after what you went through."

If that were true, he imagined he'd inherited the trait from his grandfather. Gray sure hoped he'd finally be able to talk to that cranky old Indian this morning, too. He needed answers, but Grandfather still didn't have a phone.

While he'd lived with him for ten years, going to college and learning the ways of the elders, Gray hadn't cared much about phones, either. Now that Grandfather lived alone, Gray thought maybe he should buy him a cell phone, even though neither of them wanted to jump into technology quite so forcefully. In general, the old ways were infinitely better.

But he wanted the old man to quickly be able to get in touch with him should anything happen. And Gray wanted to be able to reach him when he had a question only Grandfather could answer.

His grandfather, Stalking Moon Parker, had always lived near the progressive and relatively prosperous tribal family lands, located in southwestern Oklahoma. But the stoic old crank would have none of the modern conveniences and civilized companionship of other Comanches. He lived alone with the old ways, and far from the rest of *nemene.*

Gray imagined that by today his grandfather would've gotten the messages he'd had a neighbor hand-deliver. And Grandfather would've come to town this morning to answer a phone call placed to an old friend.

As he stepped into the kitchen of the Skaggses' main house, Gray sighed quietly. Unfortunately, his own phone privileges had been somewhat restricted lately. He could only pray that his two stepbrothers, the current bane of his existence, would be out of the house.

No such luck.

"Hey, hey, hey, looky here," the younger Skaggs brother, Milan, said as he turned from the open refrigerator door. "Take a gander at who just walked right through the back door...like he owned the place or something."

Milan Skaggs was twenty-three, and to Gray's mind he didn't amount to much. Lean and gangly at about five foot eight, the younger Skaggs boy had to physically look up to his stepbrother—which didn't do much in the way of making him any more pleasant.

At the moment Milan was grinning at him with one of his typically foolish looks. Gray tried to keep a steady and neutral expression on his face. But it wasn't easy when Milan looked so dumb, gazing up at him from under that shock of straw-colored hair.

"Don't waste your time with the Indian, Milan." Harold, the elder Skaggs brother waltzed into the kitchen, waving a small white card around in the air. "We've got more important things to attend to right now." Harold threw Gray a disgusted glance, then returned his attention to his own flesh and blood.

Gray took an involuntary step forward. But remembering where he was he fisted his hands in his pockets and froze in place, standing near the back door. Something about Harold just made him feel like a fight.

Which, come to think of it, was surprising, considering the eldest Skaggs brother's demeanor seemed so wimpy. His face always carried that pasty, drawn scowl. His nondescript brown eyes never managed to look at anyone directly, and that paunch above his belt spoke volumes about the sad state of his athletic ability.

Whatever it was that bothered Gray about Harold, he didn't want to cause any trouble with either of his stepbrothers. He'd been forced to come back here to their ranch last year after his mother died, in order to manage the mustang herd and make sure those rare Indian ponies remained pure and well. But as soon as he could afford to move them to a place of his own, he'd be gone.

Regardless of what his stepfather, Joe Skaggs, wanted…or needed.

"We've got to decide how to dress properly for this barbecue party at the Gentrys' tonight, Milan." Harold continued addressing his brother and ignoring Gray. "I don't know if regular Sunday jeans is right 'cause, besides dancing and drinking, they're supposedly showing off some new horse flesh."

"Yeah, I know," Milan replied. "Dad was talking the other day about that-there expensive Spanish *mestenos* stud the Gentrys had bought." He scrunched up his mouth and looked at the ceiling for answers. "Can't imagine why they'd be needing to compete with us, though. They've got all the money in the world, don't they?"

Mestenos stud? Gray instantly became very interested in his stepbrothers' conversation. Of course, the Indian ponies on the Skaggs Ranch belonged to him—not to any of the Skaggses. He'd inherited them legally under white-man's laws.

He couldn't imagine that the Gentry Ranch had decided to go into mustang breeding, there wasn't enough money involved for them. Milan was right for a change—it just didn't add up.

"There's some kind of shindig at the Gentry Ranch tonight?" Gray asked. He'd sure like to get a look at the neighbors' new acquisition.

Gray was not a party person. In fact, he couldn't exactly claim he'd ever been to anything resembling a party—except maybe an inter-tribal powwow. But he doubted that a rich man's Texas barbecue would be quite the same.

"Big shindig," Milan loudly answered. "Really big. Daddy says the oldest brother...what's his name, Cinco ain't it? Anyway, he's invited every eligible male in the county, looking for somebody to take his scraggly sister off his hands."

Milan grinned and hitched up his jeans. "Figure I got 'bout the best shot at it as any cowpoke 'round here."

Gray winced at the thought—and at the whiff of

Milan's rank breath he'd just gotten, but he tried to keep his features steady. Were they talking about Abby, the woman who'd rescued him and saved his life? He'd heard that she was the only daughter...the only *woman* on the Gentry ranch...except for the oldest brother's new wife. But she was definitely *not* "scraggly" looking.

Gray thought Abby was one of the most beautiful women he'd ever laid eyes on. Well, all right, perhaps she was a bit shorter than average, and her muscular body might not appeal to some, but she had the face and eyes of an angel. And...just maybe...white men liked their women to wear lots of makeup and frilly clothes. But Gray sure didn't. And he knew that Abby wouldn't wear anything that foolish. His lips began to curl into a wide grin with the thought of the strong young woman who'd saved his life.

"Don't even think about it," Harold suddenly snarled at Gray. "*You're* not going with us, brother Parker. Dad says the Gentry clan wouldn't want any ol' *Injuns* at their party. It's bad enough you embarrassed us with that snake stunt the other day. You aren't going to get a second chance to make us look stupid."

Gray knew *he* could never make the Skaggses look stupid—they did a great job of that on their own. "I thought you said our neighbors had invited *all* bachelors?" he asked Milan.

Milan ripped the invitation from Harold's hand and waved it under Gray's nose. "This here invite is addressed to 'Joe Skaggs and family.' As I recall, your name ain't Skaggs...Parker. When Dad gets done with morning chores he'll make you see you ain't wanted."

Gray pulled his fisted hands from his pockets with a jerk. Remembering just in time that these idiots were not worth the effort to scalp, he forced himself to take a step back. More than proud of his Comanche heritage, he'd never paid attention to anyone's nasty remarks or ill-informed prejudice, and he wasn't going to start now.

And if, heaven forbid, his name *was* Skaggs, he'd be duty-bound to commit suicide.

"I couldn't care less about going to any ridiculous barbecue." Gray shrugged. "But you boys better get on the stick and figure out what party frocks to wear. You've only got another eight hours or so to pretty up."

Before either of them could manage another word, he turned and strode out the kitchen door, leaving both of them sputtering and gesturing in the air. Maybe he'd go get himself a cell phone, after all. Or maybe he would try calling Grandfather at his friend's house later this morning when Abbott and Costello here were out of the house.

And after he decided what time would be best for him to show up at the Gentry Ranch barbecue.

Abby stomped up the back stairs of the main house, cussing under her breath all the way. That durn Cinco had done it again.

This time she'd been pitching in with the wranglers as they'd prepared for the barbecue. She'd helped as they dug a huge pit out behind the house, filled it with mesquite and lit the fires. They'd set up the chairs, tables and tents.

Finally, as she was helping the cooks load spits with the many sides of beef to be slow-smoked, Cinco showed up and nearly embarrassed her to death. He stood beside her at the edge of the pit, all six foot two of him, scrutinizing her.

Looking her up and down, he shook his head. "The gate just called. The first of our guests has entered ranch property. They'll be arriving within a half hour or so. I also know for a fact that some people are flying in, and they might be here anytime now."

He took out a bandanna and rubbed at her cheek until it hurt. "Are you injured or is that just dirt and ash?"

"Ow." Abby jerked her head away from his hand. "I *wasn't* injured until you started manhandling me."

The look in her brother's eyes softened and he dropped his hand to his side. "Oh, Abby Jo, darlin', why can't you be just a little more feminine? You know I don't want to hurt you. I love you. You're really a pretty girl with so much to offer. I want you to be happy."

"If you really wanted to make me happy, you wouldn't be having this party at all. You'd leave me be and let me prove my worth as a ranch foreman. Most of the other hands don't believe a woman can do the job of ranch foreman. I'm trying to win them over one at a time, and I'll never do it if you keep trying to turn me into a frilly little girl."

Cinco's eyes teared over, and Abby was horrified at the idea of him actually crying out here in front of everyone.

"You know, when you get your dander up like that," he began. "You look just like Mom used to when she was mad at one of us. Remember how her eyes used to spark just before she whacked us on the behind?"

He put his hand on her shoulder. "Your eyes turn exactly the same evergreen color as hers did."

Geez. Her brother sure was a softie inside. Too bad Abby couldn't find a way to use that so he'd back off her case and let her work in peace for what she wanted.

Besides, Abby didn't want to remember what color Mom's eyes were, or anything else about her for that matter. She'd left. Disappeared. Never returned. That was all Abby needed to remember about her.

Oh, mercy. She could see now that Cinco's eyes were about to brim right over.

"All right, brother. I'll go clean up for your party." She adjusted her work hat and put her hands on her hips. "But don't go expecting me to actually look pretty for this thing. That ain't my style."

Cinco smiled at her. "You just put on those new jeans and fringed shirt Meredith bought for you, honey, and you'll dazzle the whole of Texas."

He turned to walk away, then stopped and turned back to her. "Oh, and, Abby," he said, then grinned again. "Try to have a good time. This is your birthday. Enjoy it, sweetheart."

Abby was still muttering to herself hours later, standing right in the middle of the party. She had gone to take a shower, put on her fancy new duds and tried to get a comb through her clean, wet hair. That effort proved to be a lost cause, so she jammed her go-to-town Stetson over the mass of tangles dripping down her back and headed out to greet the nosy neighbors.

Through the whole afternoon, she'd felt like a prize calf being judged at the state fair. One pair of local cowpokes, with bobbing Adam's apples and dusty boots, ogled every inch of her body. She could almost feel them calculating her weight and whether she still had all her teeth.

After shaking hands and smiling until her cheeks ached, Abby figured she'd been pleasant enough. When Cinco tried to talk her into dancing with a few of the good 'ol boys, she decided to sneak away from the crowd and get back out to the horses where she belonged.

Lordy, but she wished for someone to save her from all this attention.

Living on the ranch all her life, Abby knew how to sneak out behind the barns without being seen. Slipping away and heading for the corrals, she skirted the show barn where Cinco was showing off their new stallion.

On the way, she figured she might like to get another look at the mustang herself before the sunlight was completely gone. So she quietly stole through the saddle barn and let the twilight hide her movements on the far side of the fencing, where the new wild Indian pony was corralled.

She found a spot next to the fence in the shadows where she could put a boot up on a rail and admire the horse alone to her heart's content. And the mustang certainly was a prize to be admired, she thought as she looked through the fence.

The parti-colored, Kiger mustang was really quite rare, and to Abby it was also quite beautiful. She'd heard Cinco describe the stallion pony to a neighbor. He'd commented on the fact that this mustang bore the prize pinto markings that the early Indians used to call medicine hat. In the waning sunlight, Abby could see its light-colored body, dark reddish ears and blotchy flanks and feet. As the horse ran the fence line, she saw the distinctive white shield on its chest.

"You're doing that pony a terrible injustice," a baritone voice suddenly said from behind her.

Abby gasped at the deep, quiet tone and sudden movement coming directly out of the shadows on her right. She turned to find Gray standing next to her, staring at the mustang who brushed past them at a gallop.

''Can't you see how agitated that animal has become?'' he demanded. ''Don't you know better than to pin a wild pony in a corral while humans stand nearby talking and laughing in loud voices? And the smell of smoke from the barbecues is making him crazy.''

''Gray.'' She laid a palm against her chest and tried to calm her agitated breathing. ''You nearly scared me to death. Where'd you come from?''

He didn't turn to look at her, but continued to study the wild pony through the fence rails. ''I came to see the new Gentry Ranch mustang.'' The corners of his mouth cracked up in what might be taken for a smile—on someone else. ''That's what this party's all about, isn't it?''

Too close. That was all she could think. The man was standing too close.

She disobeyed her body's urging to run away, but did turn her face as he had, staring out into the corral. It didn't help.

The heat from his nearness radiated right through her long-sleeved shirt. But the flush of warmth overtaking her came from deep inside, not from sizzling skin. And here she'd thought the evening had been rather cool up until now.

Hmm. Had he just asked her a question?

''How are you feeling, Gray?'' She tried to steady her shaky voice. ''I checked with the hospital, and they told me you'd gone home almost as soon as you got there. Have you recovered fully?'' She sneaked a peek at him out of the corner of her eye.

''There was no need to make such a big fuss,'' he dipped his chin. ''Your antivenom did the job. Another couple of hours rest at the shack and I could've easily made it home on my own.''

Abby wished she could see his eyes. He sounded so stilted. So far away. It was hard enough to stand here beside him when he looked so tall and tough. The Gray she'd saved had been lean and muscular, but injured he hadn't seemed so…savage.

Then he turned to face her. "The wind's changed."

She'd been wrong to want to see his eyes. So wrong.

They were black, bottomless pools that appeared to see right through her skin to the scared little rabbit hiding inside. She tried to turn her face toward the corral again, but his dark-as-pitch gaze held her spellbound and speechless.

"The stallion is quieting some. Guess everyone's gone back to the tables to eat." He seemed about ready to reach over and touch her shoulder but stopped just short and turned back toward the corral. "Why aren't you off with the rest of them at the party, princess? After all, the whole thing is in your honor."

Released from his scrutiny and slightly irritated by his words, Abby had to say something. "I'm not a princess and I don't like parties. And this one isn't in my *honor*. Far from it." She took a deep breath.

Oops. That had been a mistake. Drawing his scent deep into her lungs, she could almost taste the tangy, wild fragrance that smelled like sagebrush, mesquite and lemons. She swallowed hard, making herself choke.

He tilted his head to check her welfare. "You okay?"

She could only manage to nod until he turned back to watch the horse again.

"I spoke to my grandfather today about the…drums…from the other night," Gray said, while keeping his eyes on the horse. "I told him everything. Even about you thinking that I'd disappeared."

"Your grandfather?"

Gray fought to think past the odd erotic sensations that being near her was causing inside him. Hadn't he told her about his heritage? Guess he'd really been out of it the other day.

"You understand I am one of the *nemene*...Comanche?"

"Yes, but..."

She'd hesitated, so he quickly continued. "Grandfather is a shaman, a spiritual teacher. He's from the old school. He believes in leading people indirectly to their own answers. This time it took me aback when he actually gave me a couple of real possibilities as to what happened to us." Gray shrugged a shoulder in frustration. "Of course, he answered a few of my questions with other questions and vague distortions. But that's Grandfather."

Gray slid a glance in her direction. A few minutes ago, when he'd tried to face her, he'd felt the steam between them so strongly that he'd been forced to look away.

This was absurd. She was just another woman. And a fairly tomboyish-looking one at that.

He glanced down at her slender, firm body, and his mouth watered involuntarily. Her jeans fit tightly across her bottom, leaving him to imagine the view without the clothes. Her fringed, royal-blue shirt strained against her small breasts, making him long to feel the exact weight of those treasures in the palms of his hands.

He shook his head and glanced at the heavens to clear the images.

Gray could run ten days in the wilderness without food and very little water. He could stalk a deer without moving a leaf or ruffling the air. He'd even managed to hold his hand to the fire without burning the flesh when

Grandfather had given him the order to do so during the manhood trial.

Surely he could stand next to one young woman without succumbing to his most basic desires. Having any kind of desire, basic or not, for the wealthy heiress of the Gentry Ranch would be very foolish indeed.

She gazed quietly up at him, expectantly waiting to hear what he had to say. He forced his own gaze back to the mustang and concentrated on retelling his grandfather's words.

"After I told him about the drums and my…dream… Grandfather prayed for guidance from the ancient spirits." Gray suddenly remembered that he was talking to a white woman who did not know of the elders' ways. "You might think that what I have to tell you sounds crazy. *I* would, if I hadn't trained for most of my life to accept all the possibilities of the mystical realm to our physical environment."

Abby blinked her eyes. Out of the blue, she relived the beating drums and the hysteria of discovering that her patient had disappeared.

"I won't find anything you have to say about the other night any crazier than what I thought I saw with my own eyes." She put her arms around herself, trying to ward off an unexpected chill. "Go ahead. Tell me what answers your grandfather came up with. I'm open to anything."

She'd been an eager learner in college, taking many electives she didn't need in order to satisfy her curiosity. Abby was truly willing to hear whatever Gray had to say.

Anything to make sense of the other night.

"Have you ever heard of a vision quest?" he asked.

"Yes...somewhere. It's one of those New-Age things isn't it?"

Abby could see the smile that cracked the corners of his eyes this time, but he still didn't turn to look at her directly.

"Perhaps some modern groups have usurped the words for their own purposes. But the true vision is an ancient way of entering and communicating with the spiritual realm. To request and receive guidance from the ancients.

"It takes many years of long search and much meditation to arrive at the point of being receptive to the grand vision of life. And yet—" Gray hesitated and looked upward to the twinkling stars beginning to light up the twilight "—it appears that I have had just such a vision. You were a witness to it."

Abby didn't know what to say, so she kept her mouth shut and listened. At this point she was willing to believe just about anything.

"Grandfather says that the spirits came to tell me I am on the correct path. That saving the mustang herd and bringing them back to the ancient hunting ground is what I am destined to do."

Gray finally looked at her. "Mother and Grandfather had originally wished for me to be a tribal elder like my father. I'd been in training for many years with my grandfather, learning the old ways of the camps, the hunters and the ritual languages...until Mother died last year and left me the small mustang herd in her white-man's will."

"I'm sorry about your mother, Gray. And I sort of understand about the vision thing." She pushed aside most of the questions that nagged at her. "But what on earth does any of this have to do with me? Why did I see what I did—or didn't—that night?"

He nodded. "I didn't understand all of that, either. Grandfather says that a man must live his vision…unless there is a possibility that it was a trick of the mind or a sham of hallucination. Apparently, the fact that you heard the drums, smelled the smoke and found me gone makes you the proof of my vision. You are real, so my vision was real."

Abby scrunched her face up, trying to find some shred of truth or possibility of reality in what Gray had said.

"I know," he answered before she even knew what to ask. "It all seems impossible. You do not have the faith, Abby. You are not of the *nemene*. But sometimes your own experience will force you to become a believer."

Without warning, out of the shadows of the saddle barn, a long, lanky figure came swaggering toward them.

"Miss Gentry? That's you there, ain't it?" An obviously drunk cowboy wound his way across the yard and stopped in front of her. "I've finally found you."

Abby searched her memory for this idiot's name. "I wasn't hiding…Lewis Lee, isn't it? I've just been out here looking—"

The cowboy interrupted her words and grabbed her arm, steadying himself. "Your big brother told me I could have a dance. And the word's out you're available for more…maybe. But if it's games you're wanting…well, that's right up my alley, sugar."

The smell of beer reeking from the man's body turned her stomach. She tugged her arm, trying to break free, but that only succeeded in making him tighten his hold.

"Let her go and back away." Gray jerked at the surprised cowboy's hand, making the fellow lose his grip and balance.

Abby was startled by the authoritative tone of Gray's statement. But while she watched the drunk stagger around trying not to topple over, she decided maybe she might just use that tone to her advantage.

The cowboy finally managed to stay upright, though still leaning a bit to the left. "Hey, I know you. Ain't you some kind of kin to them Skaggs boys, Injun? They was the ones told me this little gal's free for the taking. And I mean to get mine first. What right you got to interfere here?"

He started for Abby again, but she raised her hand, palm out, and ordered him to stop. She stepped to Gray's side and slid her arm around his.

"Sorry, Lewis Lee. Looks like you and your buddies, the Skaggs brothers, weren't quite quick enough." She smiled at the way the drunk cocked his head and closed one eye, trying to put her into focus. "Let me introduce my new boyfriend...Gray Parker."

She could feel Gray tense beside her, but he remained silent. "He does have every right to interfere. We've decided to see only each other from now on. We're a...couple."

"But...but Milan and Harold...they ain't gonna like this none," the poor man stuttered incoherently.

To Abby's great astonishment, instead of denying her claim, Gray lightly shoved at the cowboy's shoulder. "Get lost, pal. It doesn't matter at all what the Skaggs boys like or don't like. The game's over here. I won. This prize has already been captured."

Four

The drunk skulked away, mumbling to himself and kicking at imaginary obstacles in his path. When he was out of earshot, Gray untangled his arm from Abby's and stepped away from her.

"Did your brother Cinco actually tell that cowpoke he could...put his hands on you?" he demanded, in a voice that sounded rougher than necessary.

"Certainly not!" Abby threw her hands on her hips and ground her heel into the dust of the barnyard. "Look. I appreciate that you bailed me out like you did, but that doesn't give you any right to question my brother or his motives. Cinco would never treat anyone like a prize to be won...especially not his own sister."

She drew herself up to her full five foot four and raised her chin. "That drunken idiot misunderstood when Cinco was trying to get me to dance and join in the party fun. That's all it was."

Gray loved the way her green eyes grew dark and blazed when she was riled up. There was a savage and passionate nature underneath that tomboy exterior; he could feel it. He wondered what else he could do to make all that heat bubble up in her eyes.

"Well…I heard my stepbrothers discussing a rumor that Cinco was trying to marry you off," he said. "That this barbecue was just about finding someone to hitch you up with…sort of like a preview inspection for a horse auction."

"What?" Abby paled and placed a hand against her chest as if she'd been struck. "No way my brother would ever do anything like that. Your brothers were lying."

To Gray's dismay the heat was gone from her eyes. In its place was icy hurt…and sadness.

"Then Cinco *doesn't* want to see you get married?" Gray had to find a way to get her talking—anything to remove that horrified look he'd managed to put into her eyes.

She drew in a breath and rolled her shoulders. "Yes, I suppose he'd like to see me married…and happy…the way he is now that he's married. But…" Abby's eyes softened a little, and Gray felt the tension start to leave his own shoulders. "You have to understand what makes my brother Cinco tick.

"When our parents disappeared at sea twelve years ago, my other brother, Cal, and I were still in school and Cinco was away at college. His whole world changed overnight. He'd always been a bit overprotective with the people and things he loved, but suddenly he was thrust into being the head of a multimillion-dollar ranch and having full responsibility for what was left of his family. He turned into a control freak whose only thoughts were of protection and trying to save all of us from ever having any more hurt. Then a few months ago, Meredith came into his life and…"

"Wait a second," Gray interrupted. "Twelve years ago? Two years before I first came to Gentry Wells. How old were you then?"

"I had just turned twelve. But to finish what I was saying about Cinco…"

"Your parents disappeared off the face of the earth when you were twelve?" He waved off the rest of her talk about her brother. "My father died of cancer when I was about that age and it shattered my life. But my mother and grandfather were there to help me through it. I can't imagine how I would have done it alone. It must have been very hard on you."

She shook her head and he could see the corners of her mouth crack up in the semblance of a smile. "No, not really. Nothing much changed in my life…except that Cinco was constantly looking over my shoulder. My wonderful grandmother had just died a few months before our parents disappeared, but she and my father had given me a good solid basis for my life."

Abby turned to look at the mustang, who stood quietly at the far side of the corral. "Both of them loved the outdoors and the animals…especially the horses. And they loved the Gentry Ranch and everything it had stood for over the last five generations.

"My father taught me to ride, rope, shoot…and to respect the land and its heritage." She put her foot on the bottom rail of the corral. "Nothing has changed that. If anything, over the past twelve years I've learned to love the Gentry Ranch even more."

Gray noted that she hadn't mentioned a word about

her mother. It struck him as odd, but he didn't really know her well enough to make a point of it.

Instead, a picture of a skinny, lost-looking little girl of fourteen came into his mind. He found that he suddenly did remember her from his one year at Gentry Wells High. But he hadn't known who she was at the time.

"I think I remember you from high school," he told her. "You were the girl that those useless teenage cowboy-wannabees used to pick on. I remember you fought back and a couple of times you gave them more than they'd bargained for."

Gray smiled at the memory of the little tomboy as she took swings at boys almost twice her size. He'd respected that girl more than any other white person he'd ever laid eyes on. So this was the grown-up version of that tiny spitfire?

She turned back to look at him. "Do you remember that you stood up for me one time? I was about to be pounded into the ground by two bullies and you stepped by my side at the last moment. You told them they'd have to come through you first."

He shook his head. He didn't remember that, but it was entirely possible. It had been all he could do not to chase off every stupid bully who'd ever been mean to her. He'd always wondered what had become of her.

"I'm not surprised that you don't remember," she murmured. "I doubt I was all that interesting to you at the time."

"You've changed a lot since then. You're all grown-up."

"So are you," she said softly.

The tone of her voice flustered Gray. He'd been lost in his memories of a little girl, but when she'd spoken in that low, sensual whisper, he suddenly realized that an energetic and frankly erotic young woman stood before him now—not the child he'd known.

He was sure Abby didn't think of herself as erotic. But to him, her strength and spunk did more to turn him on than any of the womanly wiles that others might have tried before.

And those eyes... He'd noticed that the shades of green became deeper as she became more animated. But when she went all soft, like she just had, the color turned to a pearly jade. He thought he might like that color even better than the evergreen.

Then, to his chagrin, Gray suddenly realized that what he wanted was to find out what other colors might be lurking within those fascinating depths. He wanted to see what he could do to her body to make the colors change. He wanted to touch. To stroke. To kiss and coax out every subtle shade. He wanted to mate with this woman, in every way that came to mind.

Gray swore to himself and pushed his black felt hat back from his forehead, shoving the disloyal sexual images into the back of his mind at the same time. He owed her for his life. He owed her honor...not lust.

Abby felt anxious and jittery, but she couldn't put her finger on the reason why. She knew that standing next to Gray in the deepening twilight and sharing the same few feet of splintery wood fence would be more intimate than her usual standoffish style with men. But the way his eyes darkened dangerously as he studied her was about to give her the hives. Her skin tingled, and the collar of her shirt suddenly pinched her neck.

In fact, everything felt too tight. Her breasts seemed to have swollen to twice their size so that the bra she wore rubbed unmercifully against her tender skin. And she had an ache at the juncture of her thighs that must be coming from jeans that had also mysteriously become a size too small.

She needed to get him talking about something else—in a hurry.

"You've changed so much that I almost didn't recognize you when I found you down in that dry wash," she blurted out. "Part of it is probably the hair. You used to wear it long. I'm surprised to see it so short. Why'd you cut it?"

Gray quit staring at her and folded his arms over the top rail of the fence, looking out at the mustang in the corral. "That's part of my Comanche heritage...the same as the visions."

Abby stayed quiet, listening to the flapping wings of the nighthawks, to horses snuffling nearby and to the distant sounds of the country band heating up after sunset. She wished for silence so she could listen to Gray with her heart. To hear all the things he might not say to someone so different from himself. But it probably didn't matter, anyway...because she wasn't sure she really knew how to do that.

"Cutting the hair is a sign of mourning for a Comanche brave," he told her. "I mourn my mother's death. There are many ways that *nemene* honor those that have gone forward to the land of the elders."

"What other ways?" As usual, the question came popping out of her mouth before she could really think about how nosy it might sound or whether she might really want to hear the answer.

He cocked his head and looked down at her like he wasn't sure he wanted to reveal this much to a near stranger. "You removed my shirt at the line shack to care for me,'' he said in a voice so soft it was nearly a whisper. ''Didn't you observe the 'marks' of mourning?''

''Oh. You mean the cuts on your stomach? Who did that to you?''

Gray shook his head. ''Experiencing pain...physical pain...is part of the ancient mourning ritual.''

Abby sucked in a breath. He'd cut himself? ''But you live in the modern world. Why did you have to do it?''

He turned to her then and placed his hand lightly on her shoulder. ''I believe in honoring the old way. In part, it's to make my grandfather proud of me. But mostly it's because I respect my heritage...who I am and where I come from.''

''I see,'' she said. But she didn't understand.

Gray seemed to sense her confusion. And what's more, he apparently wanted to make his position clearer to her. That, in itself, made her want to understand...and to appreciate their differences.

''Look,'' he began. ''Didn't you just tell me about how your grandmother and your father had given you a love of your heritage...a love for the Gentry land of your ancestors?''

Abby nodded. ''Yes, but... We don't deliberately hurt ourselves to mourn loved ones.''

One side of his mouth crept up into a half smile. ''I don't pretend to really understand a white man's need to possess property, either. After all, nature has given us the right to exist in this world but can destroy it all in an instant if we mistreat the land.'' He sighed and folded his arms over his chest. ''But...I have spent enough time living within your communities that I think I know what modern white man believes.''

Torn between wanting to hear his full explanation and

her growing anger at his nearly obnoxious egotism, Abby bit her tongue and stayed quiet.

"To respect your ancestors and keep their land in your possession, your kind will sometimes starve, steal and kill." His gaze grew serious, his eyes narrowed. "Have you never heard of the old range wars, or the more recent water wars? People have died in order to hold their ancestors' land, Abby Gentry."

"But that's not the same as—"

"As taking a knife to your own body in order to help dull the pain of grief?" he interrupted. "Perhaps not. But I happen to believe that deliberately inflicting pain upon yourself is far preferable to inflicting it on others."

This jerk was too much, she fumed. Had she really wanted to listen to him with her heart? Abby wished she hadn't bothered to listen at all. Just who did he think he was?

"Oh?" She sneered. "And I suppose your oh-so-noble ancestors never murdered innocent white people, burned them out of their houses or stole their children? Doesn't that count as inflicting pain on others in order to hold on to the land?"

Abby saw the flash of anger in his eyes, right before he deliberately blanked his expression and turned away from her.

"You know nothing of my people's history," he muttered over his shoulder. "Don't believe all those horror stories you've been told. You might just find that white historians have slanted the stories to their own advantage…and away from the truth."

She fisted her hands in anger but tried hard to remember that he was a guest on Gentry land…and that he'd just saved her hind end with Lewis Lee.

"Well, thanks for the lesson on Indian lore," she said

through gritted teeth. "And thanks for getting me out of that situation with the drunk. But it's late and I've got to be going now."

Abby spun around and took off toward the main house. A nasty red haze had blurred her vision, and she accidentally smacked right into the broad wall of a man's chest before she'd managed four good steps through the darkness toward the bright lights of the saddle barn.

She'd taken off in such a huff that Gray hadn't been able to keep her from nearly knocking over an old man in a flannel shirt as he came out of the growing shadows. Gray wondered if this would be yet another "suitor" that he'd have to run off.

"Whoa, Abby girl," the man said as he rocked back on his heels.

"Jake!" Abby gasped as she finally looked up. She stepped backward and steadied herself.

Gray moved cautiously toward them. He wasn't yet sure whether or not she would need his help with this man. But he wanted to be within reaching distance if things got out of hand again. It didn't matter that this hot-headed white woman didn't care to understand his heritage. His debt was not yet paid...in fact, would never be paid in full as long as he still drew a breath.

The old man placed his hands on her shoulders. "I figured I'd find you out here," he told her as she found solid footing.

"I was just going in. I've had enough party for one night," Abby replied, but temporarily stayed her ground.

The old man glanced up at Gray when he sensed his presence. "Well, hey," he said as he stuck out his hand to Gray. "I don't believe we've met before. The name's Jake Gomez. I'm foreman on the Gentry Ranch."

Gray sized him up, checking out his scuffed but polished boots, his clean jeans, new hat and wide grin. By the old man's casual and nonthreatening demeanor, Gray decided he posed no problems for Abby at the moment.

He shook Jake's hand. "Gray Wolf Parker. My stepfather is Joe Skaggs. The mustang herd on his land belongs to me."

Gray always hated saying things like that. The creatures of the earth could not belong to any man. They should be free and safe anywhere they roamed. But he'd grown accustomed to calling them "his" around white men who couldn't seem to understand the concept, and who had to put a label and a brand on everything in sight.

Jake nodded. "Your mother was Lily. Lovely woman. I was sorry to hear she'd passed away."

Gray straightened his shoulders and acknowledged the sympathetic words with a curt nod of his chin. He knew the man meant well, even though words of sympathy were not to be spoken to a Comanche brave.

Jake turned his attention back to Abby. "I think you'd better stay awhile so we can have us a little chat." He looked up at Gray and seemed to be including him.

Abby turned to Gray. "Will you excuse us, Gray?"

Jake put out a hand in a staying motion. "No. I believe Gray ought to join in our little confab. He's got a part in it."

Abby's eyebrows shot up, but she didn't argue the point. Gray could tell that she respected Jake a great deal. She appeared deferential and listened carefully to whatever he had to say. Gray wished she had as much respect for him.

Jake took off his hat and held it lightly by the rim. "I figured that all the rumors and gossip surrounding you and this here party would've died down by now, Abby Jo."

"Gossip? What are you talking about? I haven't heard anything like that," she insisted.

Jake shook his head. "The hands have been coming to me with their questions. I told them all to mind their own business. It wasn't likely anyone would've had the nerve to mention anything to you. And I thought that after tonight we could all go back to doing what we've been hired to do."

"What rumors, Jake?" Abby asked in a shaky voice.

"Well…best I can make out, Cinco told a couple of the ranchers nearby that he would like to see you settle down and find yourself a husband. That you seemed pretty lonely since you'd come home."

Abby's mouth dropped open, but she didn't make a sound.

"That was right before he sent the invites out for your birthday barbecue." Jake fiddled with the rim of his hat and looked down at the dirt. "The word spread that he was throwing this party to find you a husband. I guess the more the gossip was told, the more it seemed like he was desperate to marry you off."

"Oh, God," Abby sighed.

"Well now, missy. It weren't like anyone who knows you or Cinco believed such a thing. And I figured that you'd just suffer through this here party and it would all blow over."

Abby caught the same *but* in his tone that Gray heard. "Yeah? So how come you're out here telling me this, now that the party is nearly done?"

Jake tilted his head toward Gray. "I don't rightly

know how your relationship to this young man stands but…''

''There is no *relationship,*'' Abby broke in. ''I tended his injuries on the range…like any of the hands would've done. And I guess we're neighbors. That's it.''

Gray kept his mouth shut. The old man was leading to something, and Gray wanted to hear the rest of it.

''Seems there's a whole lot of misconceptions going round this party, then,'' Jake chuckled. ''Did you or did you not tell Lewis Lee Edwards that you were engaged to Gray Parker?''

''Engaged?'' Abby snorted. ''I never said anything like that. I just said we were dating…which we're not.'' She hesitated for a second, then hurriedly added, ''Uh, I guess I might've led him to believe we were going to make it exclusive, but…''

Gray decided it was time for him to step in. ''That man put his hands on Abby,'' he spat out. ''Said he planned to 'get' his from her. She told him we were a couple to make him go away. Nothing more.''

Jake narrowed his eyes at him. ''And you backed her up?''

''Of course. Abby apparently thought it would be simpler to tell him a story than for me to force him to leave.''

''Hmm,'' Jake murmured as he rubbed the stubble on his chin and studied them both. ''That would be a real funny story if it wasn't for the fact that everyone back at the barbecue now believes you two are going to get married. It's caused quite a commotion, I can tell ya.''

''What?'' Abby stamped her foot and threw her hands on her hips. ''What's been going on?''

Her face flushed a bright pink and her eyes were so green they looked almost black. Her fur was up, just like a riled polecat. Gray was fascinated but thought he'd better not mention any of that right now.

''Best I can piece together,'' Jake began. ''Lewis Lee came back to the party, madder 'n a hornet. He told everybody that would listen to an old drunk that you'd said you were going to marry some Injun. He even went to Cinco with his story and a demand for Cinco to set things right.''

''Set things right? What did he expect?'' Abby groaned.

Jake shrugged a shoulder. ''He was drunk and mad, missy. He wasn't expecting anything.''

''Well, what did Cinco do?''

''Cinco tried to smooth it over. Said Gray Wolf Parker was a neighbor and by all accounts a decent man.'' Jake smiled at her. ''I arrived at the party around that time and was real proud of your brother, Abby Jo. He said he thought this engagement might be a little sudden, but if you loved any man enough to marry him, then he must be very special and Cinco would welcome him into the family.''

''Oh, no.'' Abby's color faded, and even in the dim glow of the barn lights, Gray could see her miserable expression.

Jake turned to Gray and chuckled again. ''The story gets better, son. I understand that when some drunken wrangler mentioned this new rumor to your stepbrothers and began deriding them for bringing you to the party, a few swings were thrown.''

Gray fisted his hands but stayed still. ''I didn't come to the party with my *family,* Jake, but I will apologize for them. If there's any damages, I'll see to it that the bill is paid.''

''Naw. Don't concern yourself about it. Wouldn't be

a real Texas barbecue without a few punches and some black eyes the next day.'' Jake shifted to address both of them. ''Your biggest problem is what to do about the rumors and Cinco.''

Gray wasn't entirely sure what the problem was. Once everyone learned the truth, they'd have a chuckle and go on about their lives. He turned to Abby and could clearly see that she'd found some problem that he couldn't envision.

Abby swiveled to face him. ''What Jake is trying to say is that if we admit it was all a story just to get rid of Lewis Lee, not only will I suddenly be swamped with proposals from every greedy cowboy in two counties...but my brother will also look very foolish for having stood up for us. It might make him the laughingstock of this whole county.''

Gray hadn't thought about it like that. He didn't much care one way or the other about Cinco Gentry, even though the man had apparently stood up for him in public. But he didn't want Abby to be hurt by anything. And the thought of her having to fend off maybe dozens of local hired hands all figuring they'd line up for a big payoff, chilled his heart.

''What do you want to do about this, Abby?'' he asked her.

''I...'' She hesitated, looking back to Jake and then studying Gray from under the brim of her hat. ''I'm not sure what we can do. I guess Cinco and I will just have to stand up, tell the truth and take our medicine.''

Gray folded his arms over his chest and shook his head. He was about to get himself into something that was bound to work out badly. Stepping into the middle of white man's problems had never seemed like a very intelligent thing for an Indian brave to do. But this was a matter of honor.

"Couldn't we just continue to claim that we are engaged?" he offered. "Except for Jake, who would know any different? I'm sure that after a month or two things will settle down and people will stop paying any attention. Then we could simply say that we made a mistake, it's over and get back to our own lives."

Abby's eyes widened as she took an absentminded step away from him. She looked so uncertain, so unlike the Abby who took charge out on the open range, that he wanted to reach out his hand to steady her. But suddenly it occurred to him that she might be afraid—of him. So he jammed his hands in his pockets and rocked back on his heels.

"You would dictate the terms of our arrangement," he told her. "Everything we do together as a couple...or don't do...will be up to you."

Jake cleared his throat. "Well, if you want my opinion, missy, you should take him up on his offer. It would keep the pressure off your back for a while so you can continue working on the range as we planned." He smiled at her then, like a father might at a precious child. "And it would allow your brother to save face with the neighbors."

Abby straightened her back. "Okay, fine. I know when I'm cornered and out of options. It sounds like a good plan, I guess. And I was the one who started all this nonsense, after all."

Jake smiled. "No, honey. This isn't your fault. If anyone started things, it was Cinco. But his heart is in the right place, and I'm real proud of you for trying to protect him." He adjusted the Resistol on his head and half turned to go back the way he had come. "I'll leave you two now to come to your 'terms.' And I'll be seeing you back in the saddle bright-and-early tomorrow morning, Abby Jo.'' Jake ambled off into the night, whistling an old country tune.

Abby scrunched up her nose and glared up at Gray. ''You offered to do this out of some sense of duty, didn't you?''

''I owe you my life, Abby Gentry. I would do much more than play a part in a minor subterfuge to honor that debt.''

To Gray's great horror, the tough little tomboy swiped once at her nose and then sniffed. ''Dang it! Why can't the world just leave me be and let me live my life the way I want?'' The words came out like a whine, but he knew they were simply the product of raging frustration and a little bit of fear.

He reached for her then and dragged her into his arms, speaking soothing words as he wrapped her up in his embrace. ''There is no need for tears, Abby. We'll make the next couple of months go by quickly and easily. Have no fear.''

She leaned back her head and pushed at his chest with her forearms. ''You big dope. I'm not crying. I never cry.''

With that she dissolved into huge, hiccuping sobs and laid her forehead against his chest. Gray quietly kept still, mildly irritated at her display of weakness and not at all sure what else he should say, as he didn't wish to make things worse.

When she raised her head again, the dark passion of anger flashed once more in those blazing green eyes. But she made no move to be free of his arms.

''I guess I should thank you for stepping in to help,'' she said hoarsely.

All of a sudden Gray could feel her pulse as it picked up in tempo and hummed through her body. His own blood began to boil in response. Every inch of her pressed intimately into every inch of him, and his muscles tightened with the realization.

He let his thumb rub lightly under her eye, scooping away the last of the tears. But his fingers itched to rub other places. To soothe…and to stir.

Five

Abby's momentary hysteria had turned to a low, dull ache in her stomach. Gray gently cupped her face, tipping it upward so she could see him clearly. Though his dark eyes burned with an intense heat, his gaze was solid, steady.

A little overwhelmed by how close he was, she hadn't noticed before that they seemed almost melded together. But her body sure had noticed. Her thoughts suddenly detached from reality, and all she could do was feel.

The sensations were overwhelming. His rock-hard muscles under her hands. Her breasts becoming sensitive and tight. Amazingly, she even began to notice a wetness in her underwear. She couldn't remember that ever happening before. But then, she couldn't remember much of anything with Gray watching her so intently.

She let her hands roam over his powerful chest and felt his skin ripple lightly in response. How wonderfully delightful it was to feel what she could do to a man's body.

Her eyes closed tightly, as though they had been ordered to do so. But she found that, without sight, all her other senses became acute, sharpened. The heat, emanating from his body made her sweat, and she shivered as a drop rolled down her back and pooled at the base of her spine.

She made a move to lick her lips, as her skin seemed to have mysteriously combusted into fire. But the flames weren't the kind that would destroy, instead they licked and tickled her from the inside. She took a deep breath—because she wasn't sure she could remember how.

She concentrated on the sensations. The smell of leather, hay and horse surrounded her, mingling with a musky, earthy fragrance that grew stronger while Gray held her in his arms. The homey sounds of the stable as the animals settled down for the night and as the crickets called to their lovers in the star-kissed darkness gently assailed her with waves of sensuality.

Though her eyes were closed, she knew when he bent his head to kiss her. Just the lightest brush of his lips skimming across hers and she heard herself moan. She feared that making a noise would break the spell they seemed to be caught in, and she wished she could've stayed quiet. But her body, reacting on its own, left her helpless to stop.

She thought he would pull back, end the kiss. Instead Gray grabbed her up into his arms and brought his mouth down on hers in a hot, bruising onslaught. The shock almost knocked her sideways, but the explosion of pure passion blazed through her like a roaring brushfire. She sank deep into the seduction of his kiss.

Making love to her mouth, he nipped lightly at her

bottom lip until she opened and allowed his entrance. Their tongues mingled, danced, and then his began darting in and out, teasing, arousing, telling her what he wanted.

She moaned softly again, loving the intimate and sensual way the kiss made her feel. It was intense. Dizzying. Alive.

Gray's body shuddered as he heard Abby moan. Her nipples strained against his chest. He dragged her shirt from her waistband and slid his hands underneath the tails to lay his palms flat on the skin of her lower back. The softness and the moist heat was more than erotic.

She arched into him, and he used one hand to cup her bottom, lifting her against his straining erection. He wanted her to know what she was doing to him. What he wanted to do to her in return.

Her breathing was ragged. His seemed nonexistent. This flash of intense desire seared his brain, leaving him vulnerable, on the edge of madness.

From the distant reality of the world around them came the high-pitched scream of a hawk. Odd, that the hawk would hunt at night. But the shriek was enough to bring Gray out of the mist of intoxicating passion that had overtaken him.

He jerked his hands away from her skin and placed them on neutral territory, her shoulders. Watching her closely, he gently set her away from him. Her eyes were still closed, her lips moist and swollen from his kisses. The expression on her face stopped him like a splash of cold water.

Trust. She'd given herself totally over to him to do whatever he wanted.

Well, hell yes, he did want—but more important, there

was *need* and duty. What he *needed* to do was honor his debt to her—not seduce her in public.

The cool night air swirled around them, now that their bodies were apart. Abby's eyes popped open and she shook her head, trying to focus on him and what had changed.

With her eyes wide, Gray could see the vivid green had changed to sage, and the black of her pupils nearly blocked out the color altogether. A knifelike slash of molten lust dug into his gut, pushing him to take her farther into the blackness. But when he also saw the naiveté in her expression, he staggered backward—away from the temptation.

"Uh, I think..." He had to clear his throat to speak. "I think it's getting late. We should be talking about when and how we will appear together as a couple. Then I'd better be getting back." He forced himself to be practical, to make her think of the realities of their situation, as well.

Then he thought about having to face his stepbrothers and their taunting, and quickly decided practicality should also mean skipping the main house at the Skaggs Ranch tonight. He would grab a bedroll from the bunkhouse where he'd been staying and head out to his lodge on the open range. A night under the stars might be just what he needed about now.

Abby swallowed hard a couple of times. Never... never before had she been kissed that way. Oh, a couple of boys had sneaked up on her in the past when her guard had been down. But their kisses were rather tame compared to Gray's. His lips had been savage, carnal and addictive. She hadn't wanted to stop. Still didn't.

But apparently, Gray had wanted to put an end to it. He stood there casually, forcing her to think of their situation and what they'd gotten themselves into. Stepping back, to what might as well have been a million miles away, he folded his arms over his chest and put a stoic expression on his face. How could he go from passionate lover to near stranger so fast?

She wouldn't give him the satisfaction of knowing how much he affected her. "Who should know the truth about us?" she finally managed to ask. "Will you tell your family? Do you think I should tell Cinco?"

Gray's expression softened, but he still looked like a total stranger. "I won't offer my stepfamily any explanations. It's none of their business. Let them believe what they will." He raised his eyebrows and shrugged a shoulder. "But I have no idea whether you should tell your brother or not. Perhaps knowing the truth would only hurt his pride if he realized he was the one who pushed us into this charade. Then again…maybe you'd like to bring him a little pain for causing us all this trouble?"

"No. I don't want to see Cinco hurt. He's still my brother, after all. And this little story of ours won't turn out to be so awfully troublesome, will it?"

He did smile at her then, and Abby could feel the sunshine all the way down to her toes, even though the night had grown late and darkness surrounded them.

"Being engaged will be no trouble if we can find a way to work around it…without disrupting our normal routines any more than necessary," he told her. "What do you do with most of your days and nights, princess? As a matter of fact, why are you at home at all and not off jet-setting around the world?"

The wisecrack should have angered her, she guessed. In fact, she'd bet a bundle on the fact that he'd deliberately said it to bait her, to push her away and quash her lustful feelings. Well, she was more grown-up than that. She could deal with her own feelings quite well, thank you.

And his opinions really meant nothing to her in the long run, anyhow. Just as their spectacular kisses obviously meant nothing to him. She needed him for their charade. Period.

"I'm on the Gentry Ranch because it's my home." Her voice softened when she thought of the ranch. "I did go away to school, but I've decided that the ranch centers me. It's a big part of who I am. I've never really wanted to do anything else with my life but work the land…tend the herds.

"My other brother, Cal, he's the jet-setter in the family," she said, feeling the smile swell in her heart as well as on her face at the mention of Cal. "He doesn't much care for the ranch and being this far removed from the bright lights. But then, he's a star. He only comes home when Cinco bugs him enough."

"What do *you* do with your days here?"

"I work as a hired hand on the ranch," she muttered. "And you'd better be grateful that I do, too. Otherwise, you might still be out in that dry wash becoming buzzard bait."

Gray scowled, but said nothing.

Abby sighed. Dang man.

"Look," she tried again. "I like waking up under a mesquite and knowing that no matter how far I ride that day, it'll only be home that I see. I like the solitude and the beauty of the range…of the animals." She wondered if he could possibly understand her motivations, when she wasn't so sure she understood them herself. "I don't really feel alive unless I'm living out with my beautiful horses and testing my body and my determination against the elements."

"Typical white-man's philosophy," he scoffed. "It's useless for man to fight against nature for very long, Abby. I've learned that the elements possess a unique sense that most humans do not. Nature can rage when it's provoked, but there is a quiet significance to its ways. If you work with nature, it will provide. If you fight against it, it can destroy."

He finally smiled. "We'll have our so-called courtship out on the range where we both spend most of our time. I'll teach you to work with nature, not against it. I'll teach you the ways of my people. Our time together will be worthwhile."

His little speech finally set off the sparks that had been building inside her. Of all the egotistical—

"Fine," Abby spat out. "You can tag along with me as a trail partner if you want. We'll tell people that the only way we can spend time together is to do it while we work. Anybody who knows me will believe that. But you're going to have to pull your own weight."

She swirled around and headed off toward the saddle barn. "And we'll just see who teaches who, Gray Parker."

The next morning a red-hot sun beamed down on the disaster fermenting on the front lawn of the Gentry main house. Last night's party had obviously turned into more of a brawl than a celebration.

Abby had been working since before sunup with a crew of hands who all looked the worse for wear. Vern Butler sported a deep gash under his left eye as he folded chairs and stacked them in a trailer, readying them for storage. Bucky Waters's right wrist was bandaged and, with his fingers turning black and blue, he had to use his other hand to rake up dirty paper plates and broken glass bottles.

Although Abby wasn't physically handicapped, she had a different type of internal injury that kept her from giving the cleanup project her all. Her pride was suffering mightily, although none of the crew had mentioned a word about her sudden engagement or the gossip that went with it.

But then, no one had said much at all this morning. There was plenty of pain and guilt to spread around, meshing together with the melted puddles of last night's ice and the ashes of this morning's smoldering pit fires. No one seemed to want to bring up their own foolishness.

Abby found herself daydreaming about the kiss she'd shared with Gray as she folded table legs and shoveled dirt into the barbecue pits. It had been so intense. So unlike anything she'd ever experienced. One part of her wanted to find out if they would spontaneously combust like that every time they kissed, while another part of her vowed she would never again let him get that close.

Something odd had bubbled up inside her as she'd kissed Gray—something she hadn't recognized. It was like a strange sort of softness, and Abby had always thought of herself as too tough for such mush. At some point, though, the feeling turned into something more like a terrifying power, arising from deep inside her. The whole thing had been a wonder, and she wasn't sure she wanted to chance putting herself through that again.

Abby heard her name being called from across the yard and glanced up to see Cinco waving at her as he strolled over to where she stood.

"Morning, Abby Jo," Cinco said cheerfully. "I see

that being newly engaged agrees with you.'' He looked around at the bruised knuckles and hung-over expressions on the faces of the other hands. ''But maybe it's something we'd better discuss in private. Can you spare a few minutes to talk to your big brother about this sudden change of events?''

''Uh, I guess I can take a few minutes.'' She gulped.

It finally occurred to her that she might have to actually tell the brother she loved an out-and-out lie. Her stomach was in a queasy knot, and she tried to remind herself how he'd pushed her into this by his own actions.

''Aw, now don't look so forlorn, baby sister,'' he told her. ''I'm not here for any lectures. I know love is a funny thing. It's possible that a person might not ever find love in their entire lifetime. But on the other hand, on one surprising night, that same person could just look up and...bam...love smacks them right between the eyes.''

Cinco took the shovel from her hands and propped it up next to the wheelbarrow full of dirt. ''Lets go on over into the shade and I'll fetch you some water or lemonade. I've been busy since last night and I want to tell you what I've been up to.''

Abby let him drag her toward one of the tall pecan trees where cold drinks had been set out for the hands. She was a little reluctant to hear what he had to say, but she sucked up her courage and pasted on a smile.

When they'd settled into a couple of folding chairs and Abby had taken a sip of lemonade, Cinco began his little speech. She sure hoped he wasn't going to embarrass himself—or her.

''Honey girl,'' he took her free hand in both of his. ''I think I know you well enough to know that you take people at face value. That you believe the whole world must feel exactly the same way you do about things.''

She started to shake her head, but Cinco rushed to say what was on his mind.

''Don't try to tell me you aren't like that. I've known you all your life, missy, and being that way is who you are. But it's also a fine way to get yourself hurt bad. Not everyone is as goodhearted or as open as you are,'' he sighed. ''Fortunately, you have at least one big brother that watches out for your welfare.''

He grinned at her. ''Now, how much do you know about Gray Wolf Parker? What has he told you about himself?''

Abby felt irritated and uncomfortable at Cinco's words. She didn't need to know anything about Gray's background that she didn't already know. After all, they were nearly strangers and not really engaged. He'd been her hero once a long time ago, and now he lived on the ranch next door.

And Gray had been decent enough to bail her and her nosy brother out of their current mess. Didn't that mean more than anything else? What a person said and how they behaved was so much more important than what they might've done in the past.

Besides, she and Gray hadn't had a chance to talk about their pasts or to even become friends yet. But she didn't think she'd better mention that to Cinco.

''Uh, not much that's particularly important,'' she mumbled as an answer to Cinco's question.

''Just as I thought. You fell in love with who he seems to be, not who he really is.''

''No! I didn't...'' Abby halted in midsentence, reminding herself just in time not to tell Cinco that she hadn't fallen in love with Gray Parker. ''I mean...I know him well enough. We plan to spend a long time getting to know each other before we get married,'' she lied.

''Listen, sugar. I'm not trying to tell you that you've made a mistake. In fact, I'm real pleased about you and Gray. When you first found him in that dry wash and saved his life, I made a point of finding out a little bit about him. Then last night after the party and your off-handed announcement, I did some more digging. I now know quite a bit about Gray Wolf Parker and his background.''

Abby could scarcely believe what she was hearing. Cinco had investigated Gray?

''Now don't go getting that injured-party look in your eyes, missy,'' Cinco soothed. ''I did it for your safety. You forget that you are a very rich young woman. It wouldn't be too hard to imagine that a man could want to marry you to get his hands on Gentry Ranch.''

Of all the nerve. Her brother was asking for it. She ripped her hand from his and balled her fists.

''I can take care of myself, bubba,'' she said through gritted teeth.

''I know. I know. You're a real tough guy,'' Cinco chuckled. ''But even you have to admit, you're not too experienced in the love department. Think of me as your guardian angel. I'm just around to watch your back, that's all.''

Speechless, Abby slouched in her chair. There was nothing she could say to that. Nothing she could possibly tell Cinco that would stop him from blabbing everything he'd found out about Gray. She sighed in resignation and waited.

''I'll bet you didn't know that your fiancé has an MBA degree, did you? Or that up until a year ago he was in training and high on the list of potential candidates for leader of the national Comanche tribal council?''

Abby shook her head and stayed quiet. This had suddenly become worth paying attention to.

''Didn't think so,'' Cinco gloated. ''Well, seems like your boyfriend comes from a long line of chieftains and tribal elders. Sort of like royalty, you might say.''

Now that she thought of it, Gray had said something about his grandfather and his mother wanting him to be an elder. ''Do you know what kind of training he'd have to go through to be on this tribal council thing?'' she asked.

''Not entirely,'' Cinco told her. ''One of my buddies on the Internet said that these days the tribal council is mostly administrative. So I'd suppose Gray's business degree would come in handy for that. But apparently there's more to it.

''I dug up a little information that seemed to indicate there were 'tests' or trials to become a chief these days. I read that a man needs to be fluent in the language, know how to hunt without a gun and be fully aware of the tribe's history and religion…just to be considered.''

''But then why's he here…living on the Skaggs Ranch, of all places?'' she asked her brother.

Cinco shrugged a shoulder. ''I'd say that would be a good question for you to ask him. All I know is that when his mother died last year, Gray came back to Texas, to the Skaggs Ranch, and he's been here ever since.''

Cinco smiled at her with a kind of misty, sentimental look in his eyes. ''And to be honest, I'd surely like to hear the answer to your question myself, honey. I don't want to think about the possibility of you two leaving

Gentry Ranch after you marry. But I would imagine a wife should want to go wherever her husband's life took them…even if that meant leaving Texas to live near the tribal complex in Oklahoma.''

A dark cloud suddenly closed over the bright-blue West Texas sky. Abby felt a chill. Despite the fact that her brother was talking like some stupid macho chauvinist, and despite the fact that she and Gray had no *real* relationship, Cinco's words had given her a lot to think about.

Gray guided Thunder Cloud through the morning mist, following closely behind Abby on her gelding. A couple of days into their phony engagement and this was the first opportunity for them to actually spend some time together.

The tough little heiress had become a royal pain in the butt this morning, too. Spouting orders and making demands, she'd led them onto the Gentry Ranch's rangeland to finish small chores today before the spring roundup began in earnest tomorrow. It was all Gray could do to keep his mouth shut and follow her lead. *He owed her.* That particular chant had become a close companion lately, he'd noticed.

He and Abby had decided to spend most of their days on Gentry Ranch because there was so much more that needed to be done there than on the Skaggs Ranch. Gray could see to the mustang herd on Skaggs land during spare moments. After all, his stepfather ought to do a few things to earn his share of their stud fees. All Gray really needed to do was to make sure the ponies were thriving and well taken care of.

As the two riders climbed out of a low-lying and narrow valley, the sun began to burn through the remains of the predawn fog. Gray watched Abby riding ahead of him up the small incline. He could see her clearly now in the early, gray light.

She had a good seat, riding with her head high and legs barely touching the horse's flanks. He wondered how she'd look on the back of a mustang, riding free in the wind—as all riding should be.

He'd bide his time before suggesting that she change her ways, though. She wanted to be the boss of her world. But just give him some time, he'd convince her he knew what was best in this environment. Before the arrangement they'd gotten themselves into was over, he'd give her a real appreciation for his world.

Abby slowed her horse and pulled up next to an empty stock tank that was supposed to be fed by a nearby windmill. As she dismounted, Gray watched her lithe body go through the motions of jumping off her horse to the ground. Strength and agility showed in her every movement. He was enthralled by the pure beauty of woman.

"Well," she began while she untied the bundle of tools from her horse's saddlebags. "You planning on helping with the work? Or are you just going to stay astride your horse with that stoic and bored expression on your face?"

Gray slid to the ground. "I'll help."

It took a few minutes for Abby to open the gear box on the windmill and locate the offending mechanism that had stopped the water pump. She explained to him what she was doing as she worked. The mechanics of the pump were like nature, simple and pure. A lever here. A pulley there. Gray loved the elegance of its workings. The windmill belonged out here with the rest of nature's silent and productive miracles.

He lent her a hand when she was in need of a third.

They twisted and wrenched loose a couple of broken bolts, replacing what was beyond repair and fixing what could be saved.

While she concentrated on the job, Gray took a few minutes to concentrate on her. They had to work in close physical proximity as he assisted her efforts—which was no hardship at all for him. It gave him a chance to study her features up close. To drink in the smell of womanly sweat—so tangy, so compelling. To slide his arm down hers before he reached for a tool, feeling her small muscles and raw strength through both their shirts.

At one point, while she was lost in her work, Gray studied the lines and freckles on her face up close. Her creamy skin had grown pink in the sun. She was too fair for so much time on the range, he thought.

But then he lost his train of thought altogether as he spotted a tiny drip of sweat coming from under her hatband. That little bit of salty wetness rolled down her cheek, past her jawline and wound its way down her exquisite neck.

He had to catch his breath and clamp down on his tongue to keep from leaning over and tasting the sweetness of that salty sweat, to keep himself from licking that drop right off her skin. And in the meantime, tasting the honey that was all Abby.

Just at that moment the droplet slid down to her collar and disappeared underneath to the rounded depths that were hidden by her denim work shirt. Gray wanted to follow it there. He wanted to place his lips where that drop had gone. To satisfy himself—and to excite her.

"Well, that takes care of this job." Abby stood and dusted off her hands. "Want to take a little break? I could stand some coffee. You want water?"

The windmill creaked a few times as the winds stirred

it into life, and then the nearly silent shifting of the breeze was all Gray could hear. In another minute the water bubbled into the tank. He was grateful for the distraction.

"Coffee would be good," he told her.

Abby used a little of the water to wash her hands and face, and Gray followed suit. The water, though not particularly cold, was cool and clear. They let the air dry them off while she replaced her tools and retrieved the coffee thermos from her saddlebags.

Before Gray could take his second sip of coffee, Abby's cell phone rang. She took it from her shirt pocket and answered the call.

When she'd bidden goodbye to the caller, she turned to explain to Gray. "That was Jake on the phone. He's found another chore that needs doing this morning. And we're the hands nearest to the problem, so we're elected."

Gray took a last sip, nodded to her and splashed the dregs left in his cup onto the ground.

"This whole section has been newly restrung with barbwire." She waved her arm in a wide arch. "Remember when you said your horses were having trouble with our fences? Well, we've replaced every piece of wire between our two ranches since then.

"Now it seems that some of the new wire is failing. Not holding up. Doesn't seem right. I helped put most of it in myself. No reason for it not to be sound."

"Maybe the wire was bad," Gray volunteered.

"Maybe. We'll see. We're going to ride up the fenceline for a few miles and check."

Twenty minutes later Gray found himself following behind Abby once more while they rode slowly, checking the Gentry fence as they went. The sway of her hips and the straight-as-an-arrow strength of her spine fascinated him.

She was getting to him. Seeping under his skin. He vowed to find a way to ignore what he felt when he was with her. It wouldn't do for him to give way to such lust.

As he tried to tear his eyes away from her, Abby's gelding suddenly reared up. Gray watched as she held her seat and tried to calm her mount. But the horse pawed the ground and bucked sideways as if something was in his path that had panicked him.

The more Abby tried to stay with him, the more it seemed that the horse was determined to jerk away. The horse's eyes rolled back in his head and he snorted wildly, nostrils flaring.

Then Gray spotted the piece of loose wire that had by now wrapped around the horse's foreleg. He slowed Thunder Cloud and jumped to the ground, running toward the gelding as fast as he could. He tried to yell a warning to Abby, but the noise and confusion blocked out his words.

And he got there too late. When he was within a few feet, Abby's horse twisted its body nearly in half and lost its footing.

To Gray's shock, the gelding began to fall, taking Abby with him. Gray wanted to shut his eyes to the tragedy that was unfolding before him, but he couldn't look away.

He could only hope that maybe, because she was so athletic and sure of herself on horseback, Abby would be able to jump clear. That she wouldn't allow herself to be pinned beneath her own horse as it went to the ground.

Sure enough, Abby sprang away from the horse's

back as the gelding slipped. But her timing and position were all wrong. Instead of jumping to the left, she went over the horse's head and landed on his right.

As if in some disastrous slow-motion video, Gray watched Abby land, arms and legs askew, directly on the barbwire fence. In one horrific moment, the fence gave slightly under her weight and then made, what Gray thought must've been, one of the worst sounds he'd ever heard.

The snapping noise as the wire popped loose from its post was loud enough to be heard twenty miles away. Gray was powerless to do anything to stop it.

The taut wire's recoil was swift, unyielding, and with Abby directly in its path—potentially deadly.

Six

Gray was at her side the instant the recoil stopped. ''Abby!''

He heard Abby moan and thanked the powers that be. But he couldn't touch her. The wire had wrapped around her body, holding her in a barbed cocoon. Blood flowed freely from her skin, and was even now in the process of slowly coloring everything with a wet scarlet blanket.

''Don't move,'' he shouted. ''Abby, do you hear me? Don't move.''

''The gelding,'' she groaned softly. ''Help the horse.''

He ignored her and bent to study the wires holding her captive. ''Let me free you first. The horse can wait. Please be still.''

No major arteries seemed to be cut. The closer he looked, the more he realized that blood wasn't spurting from any of her wounds. All the places of cut flesh that he could see were leaking blood, not gushing it. But there were so many places.

She turned her head slightly, and Gray saw the gash on her cheek widen with a sickening rip of flesh. "The horse first," she whispered.

He wanted to shout at her to be reasonable. To let him cut the barbs away from her skin right now. But then he saw the determination in her half-closed eyes, and he knew it was no use. Abby would only be still if he made sure the horse was all right first. Fear for her well-being warred with his own need to help any creature that could not help itself.

"Okay. All right. I'll see to your horse. But you stay absolutely quiet. No more talking. Don't even blink."

Gray rushed to the gelding. The poor animal lay struggling on the ground where he'd fallen, and the more it flailed the worse the loose wire tangled around its leg. Things were desperate for the horse. Every time it moved the barbs dug deeper, and blood had begun to spout profusely from the wounds.

Gray spoke in the language of his Comanche forefathers. He didn't know if that might help calm the animal, but it wouldn't hurt. It also gave Gray something to think about while he tried to ease Abby's tool bag from the pack attached to the gelding's saddle.

Luckily for Gray, the tool bag was situated on the left side of the struggling horse's body. If it had been on the right, between the horse and the ground, Gray would never have been able to reach it.

He spoke to the gelding in as soothing a voice as he could manage while he ripped the tool bag open and found the wire cutters. When he had them in his hand, Gray realized he couldn't cut the horse free while the animal still kicked and fought with its barbwire captor.

He knew he had to do something else to calm the horse, so he moved to Thunder Cloud's side and ripped a buckskin rag from his packs.

Thunder Cloud was watching the injured horse with concern and that gave Gray yet another idea. "Help me to help your brother, Thunder Cloud," he begged the mustang. "I will save him, but he must stay quiet."

Gray gingerly placed the rag over the downed gelding's eyes at about the same time that Thunder Cloud made a loud snuffling noise deep in his throat. The gelding reacted immediately to the darkness and the call from his brother horse, settling into a tense calm and allowing Gray to remove the wire prison.

When the barbs had been cut away and dragged off and hidden under a bush, Gray removed the rag from the gelding's eyes. The horse was on his feet again a second later. Gray quickly tied the rag around the gelding's foreleg in an effort to temporarily stanch the blood flowing from the cuts.

Without taking so much as another breath, Gray was back at Abby's side. "The gelding's up. We can tend his wounds later. I'm going to cut you free now. Keep your eyes closed and remain as quiet as possible," he said in a too-harsh tone.

Abby made no sound or movement, and for a second Gray wondered if she'd passed out. But then, as he studied the wire that had wrapped around her face, he noticed her eyelids jerking while she obviously fought to keep them closed. She was still conscious and still tightly wrapped in the ball of wires. His heart thumped in his chest with fear for her.

Why couldn't this have happened to him instead? He'd trained for surviving great bodily hurt. Had practiced closing his mind off to the pain. Had literally spent years learning to remain perfectly still while he sat awaiting the hunt.

But this calamity had befallen the strong little female of Gentry Ranch. Had happened to the woman who'd saved his life. To Abby. So alive, so beautiful and so animated. His vision blurred as he looked down at her, and when he swiped at his eyes, he found wetness there. He set his jaw and picked up the wire cutters again.

A great aching anguish stole over his spirit, rendering him less effective in his efforts to help her. He closed his eyes for one still second and prayed to the ancient elders for assistance. *Please, fathers, help me to see not the injured woman but only the work that has to be done. Give my hands strength and stable movements. Let me save her life as she saved mine.*

When he opened his eyes again, he saw a tiny gap in the knot around her head. With one hand, he held the wire tightly, while with the other he gently made one cut directly over the gap. He heard a snap but felt no further recoil or tightening. It had worked. He'd found a way to cut away the tangle without making the situation worse.

Gray set about making cuts at every juncture where he found a gap. He had to concentrate only on the wire itself, because each time he glanced at Abby's bloody skin where the barbs still clung to her, his heart ached and he was afraid his hand would slip.

He freed her from most of the prison easily enough, but some of the barbs had latched agonizingly onto her skin. They'd dug themselves deeply into Abby's flesh, as terribly as they'd done to her gelding.

Finally there was nothing for Gray to do but begin the slow process of extracting what was left. "Abby. I'm about to start removing the barbs. It'll hurt much more than it has already, I'm afraid."

He heard a tiny groan for her answer, and he knew her muscles must ache from remaining still for so long. From his own experience, he knew her muscles might also start cramping up anytime now.

"I'm going as fast as I can," he told her. "Stay with me. Don't give up yet. If you'll just be strong and quiet for a little while longer, it will all be over."

Gray began with the ugly laceration on her cheek. The barb had gashed its way across her face and buried itself deep, right under her eye. Another half an inch and she might've been forever blind in that eye.

Oh, so carefully, he worked the barb free of her flesh. But then he had to do something to stop the blood from flowing back out of the gash. He jerked his cotton chambray shirt off and ripped it into strips. His shirt might not be the cleanest right now, but it was the fastest way to keep her life's force from spilling to the ground.

He worked on the rest of the attached barbs with both hands, using the wire cutters and some needle-nosed pliers he'd found in Abby's tool kit. Every time he pulled a barb free, blood spouted from the wound. Gray wanted to wince with each nasty removal, but he remained stone-faced and concentrated on his work. This was for Abby. He owed it to her.

By the time he'd worked down and around her body, and all that remained encased in barbs were her legs, the sweat was pouring from his brow and down his back like rivers of angry lava exploding from a volcano.

"You have to keep your body still for a while longer yet," he said, with a lot more assurance than he felt. "But you can open your eyes now and talk to me a little. I have to know how you're doing."

Abby opened her eyelids, squinting at her surroundings. He saw the great pain reflected in her gaze, and knew the tremendous strength she'd brought to bear in order to maintain her calm. His heart wrenched at how she'd managed to stand all this pain without crying out.

Gray felt pride and admiration for her control begin to swell in his chest. At the same time, though, her pain started to seep into his own body, making every inch of him burn with sympathy.

Instantly Gray remembered who she was. Damn strong-willed white woman. How irritating it was that she'd gotten to him like this. It was fine for him to honor his debt to repay her in all possible ways. But this strong attraction was simply out of order.

"Wait. Get the first-aid kit from my pack," she mumbled hoarsely.

"Shut up, Abby," he told her. "Stop giving orders and let me help you."

He turned away from her and carefully stood, needing a minute to get ahold of himself.

An agonizing twenty minutes later, Abby was free, and Gray had slathered her body with a whole tube of antiseptic ointment, wrapping as much gauze around her arms and legs as he'd dared. Most of the wounds had stopped bleeding profusely, but continued seeping through the bandages in a few places.

"Can you reach my cell phone?" she mumbled through gritted teeth.

He glanced over at her inert body, and kicked himself for not having thought of the phone a long time ago. Abby's clothes were in shreds. Even the heavy jeans she'd worn had ripped with the outrageous onslaught of the pressurized barbs. He remembered that the phone had been in her shirt pocket, but when he looked, her practical white bra, soaked in dried blood, was all that was left to cover her chest on that side.

Looking quickly around the ground nearby, he found her phone a few feet away. "Who should I call?" he whispered with as much control in his voice as possible.

"Just hand it over," she demanded in a weak voice.

"There you go again," he winced. "Giving orders. You can't hold a phone. Look at your hands."

She moved her head and groaned.

Damn it. Damn her. Why did he let her push him like this?

"Tell me how to reach the ranch," he pleaded. "I know it's one-button dialing. But which one?"

"Number three."

Gray managed to contact the ranch foreman but all the while his hands shook almost uncontrollably and the metallic smell of blood filled his nostrils, nearly choking off his words. When he'd relayed their position, Jake told Gray that the paramedics' helicopter would be there shortly.

After he'd put away the phone, Gray didn't know what else to do for her. He was half-afraid to touch her. Afraid he'd make the bleeding worse.

But she looked so pitiful lying there on her side, trying not to breathe too hard for fear of the pain. She seemed so…alone.

As gently as he could, Gray lifted her head into his lap and took the least of her injured hands into both of his. "Abby it's going to be okay. The paramedics will fix you up and take away the pain while they fly you to the hospital. You'll see. They'll treat you like royalty, I promise."

She blinked and moaned. He wished he could do something more for her comfort.

''Did you finish tending my gelding?'' she whimpered.

''Not yet.''

''Do it now. I want to know that he's okay,'' Abby told him.

''Damn it, woman,'' he began, but thought better about finishing the sentence. He'd wanted to tell her to stop ordering him around. To be quiet and let the blood clot. ''Just relax,'' he mumbled instead.

He was angry and not being rational, he knew. No rational person would expect her to be civil while she was still in all that pain. He'd always prided himself on being reasonable and logical even in times of great stress. But every time he looked at her wounds, he couldn't seem to help himself. He wanted to strike out at something, at someone—not at all the kind of attitude a Comanche chief should have.

He took a deep breath, and when he was finally able to assemble his words into a more rational statement, he said, ''Your horse will be fine. As soon as the paramedics get here, I'll medicate and wrap his leg wounds. Now lie still.''

Abby closed her eyes…breathed softly. Gray did the same, all the while praying for guidance from the ancient ones.

Abby opened her eyes and tried to focus on her hospital room. Her gaze finally landed on her brother, Cinco, sitting in a chair next to her bed. His eyes were closed and he looked tired.

She swallowed hard and suddenly realized how really dry her throat was. Turning her head to look for water, her glance landed on a dark object in the far corner of the room. Then she saw clearly that it was Gray, leaning back against the wall with his arms folded over his chest and his eyes closed, too.

Didn't these two men have anything better to do than doze off in her room? She figured she'd been in this bed for a day or two since being brought here by the paramedics, and though the doctors had given her enough medication to make her sleep through the bulk of the pain, she did remember that both Gray and Cinco had been in her room for much of the time.

She tried to clear her throat to ask for water, but all that came out was a tiny squeak. It was enough for both men to open their eyes and come to attention in a hurry.

"Abby Jo," Cinco declared. "You're awake. How're you feeling?"

"Thirsty," she mumbled over her swollen tongue. "Could I have some water, please?"

Cinco picked up a plastic cup and straw and put it to her lips. "Sure, sugar. Here ya go."

She managed a few good swallows, feeling a whole lot better right away. "How's the gelding? Did he make it okay?"

Gray piped up from his position next to her bed. "Your horse got through in much better shape than you did. His bandages will be off tomorrow, and then he'll forget the whole ordeal. You'll be on his back again as soon as you're able."

Well, at least that was good news, she thought. She tried to shift her position and quickly found that she was indeed in much worse shape than the gelding. Both of the men in the room moved to help her sit up.

When her pillows had been fluffed and the bed raised so she could see, she noticed that Gray's expression seemed rather stark. Or perhaps *wary* would be a better word. She turned to Cinco and found the same look in his eyes right before he softened them to smile at her.

"What's been going on while I was out of it?" she asked.

Gray and Cinco exchanged dark, darting glances, making her curiosity jump to attention.

"Honey girl," her brother began. "How much of your 'accident' do you remember?"

Abby didn't much care for the emphasis he'd put on the word *accident,* but decided she'd find out what was going on in due time. "I'd rather not remember any of it—especially not the part about those two hundred stitches I was forced to endure. But I guess most of it is in my memory banks somewhere. Why do you ask?"

"Well..." Cinco sat forward in his chair and leaned his elbows on his knees. "Something didn't sit right with me about that loose wire on the ground. None of our hands would be so careless."

"Come to think of it, you're right. Everyone who works on the Gentry knows what barbwire can do to horseflesh," she hesitated, swallowed again. "Or to human flesh."

"Exactly," Cinco said softly. "So I organized a little investigation. Jake and I double-checked all the new fencing the ranch has put up over the past month."

He stopped speaking, glanced over to Gray, then took a breath. "There were at least six places where we found loose wire on the ground...most of it looked as if it had been placed or...planted...there."

"Planted?" she blurted. "As in deliberately, you mean?"

Cinco nodded. "'Fraid so, sugar."

"But who would do such a thing?" She forced herself

to maintain some calm. With every inch of her body still in pain, she tried hard not to jerk around too much.

"That's one of our biggest questions. But not the only one," Cinco told her. "Besides the loose wires, we also found some of the fence strands had been loosened at their posts. Many of them were only being held together by a tightly strung thread."

"But...but that sounds like someone deliberately wanted to cause an accident," she sputtered.

Cinco grinned at her then, but the expression in his eyes was still grave. "That's my guess, missy. But I'm not sure I'd call what happened to you an accident."

"What would you call it, then," she demanded.

"Attempted murder," Gray broke in with a voice sounding way too quiet, way too sober.

"Oh, my God." Abby sank back into her pillows and wished she could disappear. This couldn't be possible.

She reached for glass of water with her one good hand and took a couple of big swigs. "Then you two don't think my accident was just some prank gone wrong?" Turning, she questioned Cinco. "You're sure it wasn't vandalism like we had the last time when Meredith was in hiding?"

"No, sugar," her brother said gently. "Someone deliberately wanted to injure or kill one of the people working on Gentry Ranch."

"But why?" she cried.

Gray came closer to the bed. "Good question. We've all been asking the same thing. Jake and the sheriff have come up with a possibility." He stood straight and tall so she couldn't see his eyes from this angle. "They think it's more a question of *who* someone would want to hurt on Gentry Ranch."

"Who?"

Cinco took the cup of water from her and laid it on the table. "Jake suggested that one of the cowpokes who'd thought he deserved a chance at marrying you might be angry enough and jealous enough at the thought of losing out to…to want to see you dead." He looked at Gray, then turned back and picked up her hand. "He thinks it was you they were after. Or, if not you, then Gray."

Both Cinco and Gray stood, silently waiting for something. For her to become hysterical, she supposed. She could see them holding their breaths, probably waiting for her fear to show up in the form of tears. But she didn't feel like crying.

The only thing Abby felt at the moment was red-hot anger. She was downright furious.

She ripped her hand from Cinco's. "You mean to tell me that Jake and the sheriff think some lovesick cowboy would deliberately take a chance on maiming or killing an innocent horse in order to get back at me…for becoming engaged to Gray?" Her voice had gone up two octaves, but she couldn't help that. "I don't believe it."

Cinco and Gray looked at each other and then back at her. Each of them took a step away from her bed.

Cinco was the first to find his voice. "Now, Abby Jo. I know you won't want to accept this, but we've gone through every motive we can think of. Your engagement caused so much consternation in the county that it seems to be the only reasonable answer."

"Well, dang it all to hell" was the only remark she could think to make. She'd be throwing something, too, if her pitching arm wasn't so sore at the moment.

Her brother chanced a little more of her ire. "That's not all of it, sugar," Cinco said warily. "The sheriff is afraid you're still in danger. He's had a deputy sitting outside your door while you sleep. He wants to assign a man as your bodyguard permanently…or at least until we figure out who did this.''

''No chance, bubba,'' she said through gritted teeth. She wanted to scream…shout…find the idiot who hurt her horse and wring his neck, but she didn't want to be saddled with a sheriff's deputy. ''You tell the sheriff that I said to shove—''

''I'll stick with you, Abby,'' Gray said.

He turned to Cinco. ''It might be me they're after, right?''

Cinco nodded. ''Yes, but…''

''Then Abby and I will stay together and protect each other. I don't trust anyone else to watch my back the way I trust her.''

Abby's heart twitched at Gray's words. No one had ever before said they'd trust her with their life. She looked up to see him gazing at her so sincerely she thought she might die from the swelling of her heart.

''Yes, and I trust Gray to protect my back, too,'' she told her brother. ''He already took care of me once. We don't need bodyguards. We have each other.''

Cinco shook his head but didn't argue. ''I'll talk to the sheriff. See what I can do. In the meantime—'' he picked up his hat and headed toward the door ''—you look like you need to rest, missy.

''The doctor said that even though the bulk of the sutures won't be taken out until next week, if you feel strong enough, there's no reason you can't go home tomorrow. Meredith can bring you some clothes for the trip to the ranch. She'll be in to visit you later this afternoon. Tell her what you'll be needing then.''

Cinco opened the door and turned back to her. ''I'm doing everything I can to find out who did this to you, honey. No one on the ranch will rest until we find him. But you have to help us by not taking any chances with your own safety. Listen to what Gray and I tell you, will you?''

Abby nodded to her brother, but she was already wondering how soon she could get back to work on the range.

''Uh, walk me down to the truck, will you, Gray?'' Cinco asked. ''I need a word.''

''Sure. Meet you at the elevator in a minute.''

Gray turned back to Abby when Cinco closed the door behind him. ''I won't be gone long. The sheriff's deputy is still sitting outside.'' He picked up her good hand and tenderly placed his lips against her bruised knuckles. ''Don't worry, sweetheart. We're going to be just fine. We have right and honor on our side...not to mention the ancient spirits of my vision.''

The softness of his kiss and the tenderness in his eyes dazzled her. Woozy, she closed her eyes and sighed.

''I'm not worried, Gray.''

He carefully set her hand back down on the bed and quietly left the room. Cinco wanted to give him some instructions on how best to protect his sister, Gray knew. But her brother shouldn't have any qualms in that department. Gray hadn't taken all those lessons in survival for nothing. No one alive would be able to come at him with a sneak attack, now that he knew the threat was out there.

Once outside, Cinco did talk to him about protection, but Gray managed to convince him that he could take care of any strike that might come on the ranch. Then Cinco gave him a few instructions on where he thought Abby could go to be as safe as possible. Gray listened politely and made a few mental notes. When, finally,

Cinco was in his truck with the motor running, Gray stood beside the window to hear his last-minute comments.

"One more thing, Parker," Cinco began. "I wanted to thank you for everything you did for my sister out on the range the other day. If you hadn't been there..." He coughed, clearing his throat. "Personally, I don't know how you remained so calm in the face of such disaster, managing to pull out all those barbs and waiting for the helicopter." Cinco shrugged a shoulder and continued. "If that had been me, looking down at the love of my life lying there bleeding and battered, I don't know that I could've been so rational and levelheaded."

A few minutes later Gray watched as Cinco pulled the truck away from the curb, then he turned to look up at the hospital where Abby lay sleeping. No, he thought, contemplating Cinco's words and remembering back to his own. If he were in love with Abby, he couldn't possibly have been so rational out there on the range in the face of all her pain. Ha! *Rational* had been his exact word, too.

The truth was...what he did or did not want made no difference. He couldn't love a white woman. Respect, yes. Friendship, yes. Sex...perhaps. But with real love came lifetime commitments. As far as Gray was concerned, his life was already committed to the *nemene*. When he did take a wife, it would be a squaw that was chosen by the elders of the tribe for his bride.

Over the next few hours, sitting by her hospital bed and watching her sleep, Gray had to remind himself several times that it was certainly a damn good thing that he was a rational man and didn't really love Abby.

Yes, indeed. Love would only complicate everything.

Seven

Abby gingerly climbed aboard the back of a mare and breathed in the mellow amber air of early spring. She was so grateful to feel the sunshine, nicely warming her insides after ten days of recuperating at home, that she didn't even mind the few minor aches still irritating various parts of her body.

"You're sure Jake said I wouldn't be allowed to help out with the roundup?" she asked Gray, who assisted as she adjusted her saddle.

Gray had been by her side constantly for the past ten days. Of course, for most of that time, she'd been asleep or at the doctor's office, having the remainders of the sutures pulled from her healing skin. But regardless of where she'd been for all those hours and days, he'd stuck with her…just as he'd promised. This was to be her first day on horseback since the incident.

Gray shook his head. "No, Abby. You know the doctor doesn't want you overexerting yourself until you have the plastic surgery on your face.''

Her gloved hand immediately flew to her left cheek, to the worst gash from her encounter with the barbs. She was much happier when she could forget about it. But now, with Gray watching her closely, she remembered how angry the red mark looked in a mirror as it streaked across her face.

It was at times like these that she almost wished she had let the sheriff put his guard on her, instead of having Gray constantly by her side and witnessing her ugliness. But that weak wish only lasted a moment.

She wanted to look good for Gray, a feeling she'd never experienced before. The ugly scar across her cheek bothered her, but it didn't seem to bother him too much. If he could ignore it, so could she.

Besides, she was more than a little taken with Gray and wanted to keep him by her side so she could continue to drink in the way his jeans clung to his thighs…and the way his muscles strained the sleeves of his shirt. When she'd been resting at home, struggling to sleep through the hazy pain, she'd remembered his tenderness and the way he'd worked so quickly to not only save *her* life but the life of her horse. He'd been careful and sure, if a little cranky. The doctor told her that he'd probably saved her from any worse scarring.

The memory of his golden skin, gleaming and slick in the hot sun, came back to tease her. Even with all her pain and fear that day, rusty shreds of the memory of his tenderness—*and* the naked muscular arms he'd bared to bind her wounds—gave her enough of a thrill to distract her through the worst of times.

Gray spoke and brought her back to the present with a jolt. ''Let's just stay with our plan today,'' he said.

"We'll take a nice slow ride over to the Skaggs Ranch, check on the mustangs, and then I'll take you to visit my lodge for a picnic lunch. Okay?"

Abby nodded as she adjusted her seat astride the mare. Dang. It was good to be back in the saddle. Even if it was only for an easy, morning ride.

As she and Gray rode toward his stepfather's ranch, Abby tried to find a way to make the time seem less tiresome and thought of some questions she'd been meaning to ask. Since the doctor insisted they walk their horses instead of taking her usually faster gait, she figured this might be a good time for her to talk to him without interruption.

"Uh…tell me more about the mustangs. I heard you say they belong to you. I don't understand. I thought they belonged to your stepfather, Joe Skaggs. That he must've inherited them from your mother."

Gray lifted his work hat and shoved a hand through his hair. She saw that he'd been letting his hair grow. The thick, black strands curled around his ears and had already started to lengthen down his neck. A little itch started to grow in the base of her spine, and she turned her head to find something else to stare at.

"Mustangs are creatures of the earth and the Great Spirit," he told her in a deep, quiet voice. "They cannot belong to any man. We can adopt them, take care of them, help them survive in the wild if we wish, but no one can own such a wild and free thing."

She swiveled slightly to find his eyes, needing to see the expression on his face. But he'd replaced his hat, and the brim cast a dark shadow over his eyes.

"Unfortunately, white men believe only in the power of possession," he said in a gruff tone. "So, legally, I suppose, the answer to your question is, yes, the herd belongs to me.''

He looked out at the open range in front of them—at the scruffy brush, the gnarled mesquite and the small dots of a few tall oaks in the distance. ''My mother left them to me in her will. She'd told Joe Skaggs when he married her that the mustangs must stay in the hands of the *nemene.* That my father had wanted me to be their caretaker when she could no longer manage.''

Gray shrugged his shoulders. ''I guess my stepfather wasn't altogether happy about not keeping control of the herd. He'd been made trustee of my mother's estate but that wasn't enough. He petitioned the court to change the terms of the will, but he didn't get very far, even though I couldn't afford a lawyer to represent my interests. Made my life miserable for several months, I can tell you, and just after I'd buried my mother, too.''

''Oh, Gray, I'm sorry. But why did he want control of the herd so badly? They're lovely, free-spirited and basic, but...''

''Yeah, I know. There doesn't seem to be much money involved in raising mustangs.'' He hesitated, looked over toward her, then turned to the front again and continued. ''Except, people in the know understand that a few rich gentleman ranchers like having exotic animals to show off to all their friends...and are willing to pay big bucks to own them.''

He took a breath, and it hit Abby what he'd said. ''You mean like Cinco, don't you?'' She felt the flare of anger flash over her like a sudden rainstorm. ''I'll have you know that Cinco is not a 'gentleman' rancher. He works hard. We all do. He just does his work mostly from a desk, that's all.''

She tried to breathe evenly, counting to ten in silence.

"And Cinco bought that new medicine-hat mustang as a favor to a friend," she blurted fiercely. "An old buddy of his had gotten himself into deep debt, needed to sell off the bulk of his stock. Cinco was afraid that the mustang might be sold to the wrong type of person so he bought it himself. He thinks it's a beautiful animal. So do I."

Gray turned, and she knew he was studying her from under the hat's brim. "Yes, I believe you do."

He hesitated one more second, as if trying to decide what to say. "I've allowed my stepfather to sell some of the ponies to a few special people, and we've sold the mustangs' services in stud a few times, as well," he finally admitted. "But as far as I'm concerned that's only a temporary measure. It enables us to raise enough funds for Joe to pay down his debts and to keep the mustangs healthy.

"As soon as I can save enough up for range land of my own, the herd and I will be moving far away from Joe Skaggs. I want the mustangs to be free-roaming the way nature intended...and not used for some white man's pleasure. I may allow them to be shown for instructional or historic purposes someday. But they should forever be available for all people to enjoy, not just a few."

"They're that important to you?" she probed somberly.

"They are that important to the *nemene*. Mustangs are our heritage. Throughout history we've been known as Lords of the Southern Plains, renowned for our skilled horsemanship. Comanches were the first people to learn about horse breeding, they were the first and best horse traders in the West and, because of the mustangs, nearly invincible warriors on horseback."

Cinco had been right, she thought, when he'd predicted that Gray would eventually leave the area in order to be with his tribe. Hadn't Gray just said that he would be moving far away with the herd as soon as he saved up enough money?

"The history and fate of the *nemene* and the mustang are intertwined," Gray added after waiting a beat. "It is the will of the ancient elders that I am to be their caretaker and bring this herd back to its great numbers, relocating them to their original homeland."

"Well, I guess I understand that," Abby told him. "I know what it feels like to love a horse so much that it becomes the most important thing in your whole life. To help bring a horse's foal into the world. To have a horse as your only friend and companion day in and day out. And even to have a horse give his life for yours."

She was riding Patsy again today, and she remembered how the mare had gone above and beyond her duty when they'd saved Gray from the dry wash. Abby reached over, gave the mare's neck a few pats.

Gray nodded. "You understand part of it. Enough to know that I cannot go against who I am. I must see to it that the mustangs are free to range on the ancient hunting grounds. Some things are expected of me, and I must live my heritage."

They'd arrived at the gate between the Skaggs and Gentry lands, and Gray dismounted to lead both horses through to Skaggs property. Then they rode along in silence, each lost in their own thoughts, their own backgrounds.

When Gray slowed his mustang a little while later, Abby looked up to see a four-sided enclosure with a thatched-style roof and cowhide outer walls. It didn't have windows, but the roof did have a pipe that looked as if it might be connected to a cooking stove.

"Oh. A modern teepee?" Abby wondered aloud.

"No." Gray advised. "It's called a lodge."

She wanted to see the rest of this wondrous structure, wanted to see for herself how it was made. "We're going in, right?"

Gray slid off the back of his mustang. "Yes. You need rest now."

His words irritated her a little. She should know best what her own body needed. He didn't have to tell her what to do or when to do it.

But as he left his mustang and moved toward her, the irritation fled and was quickly replaced by admiration. His loose and lanky build, his back straight and strong, gave him such a natural manner, as if he'd been carved right out of the earth and still belonged to it.

How could she stay annoyed with such a fantastic human being? He was beautiful, strong and honorable…and he loved horses. It was really too bad that he didn't understand her love and need for the land. Too bad he wouldn't be around so she could admire him for the next twenty or thirty years.

Gray wasn't too sure about bringing Abby to his lodge and this far away from the main house. But he was following Cinco's instructions and staying off her normal haunts on Gentry land. Abby's brother had made him promise to guide her to places that she seldom visited—in order to throw off any stalker that might know her habits.

He watched Abby as she started to swing her leg backward over the horse, readying herself to dismount the way she always did. But she hesitated in midswing and winced.

"Hold on," Gray scolded her. "Let me help you down."

The expression on her face at his words told him everything. She was in pain but furious with her body for betraying her. Well, he would help her—no matter what she wanted.

"Sit still a moment and let the pain ease," he told her as he stepped up directly beside her horse.

When she'd stopped fidgeting, he began to speak to her in soft, caressing tones—the same as he would an injured pony. "Breathe, princess...."

She looked at him sharply and he felt himself smiling at her spunk.

"Yes, I'm sure you know how to breathe the same as I do. But you weren't just then. You were holding your breath, holding in the pain instead of letting it go." He reached over and gently put a hand on her arm, hoping to give her some quiet strength.

Abby's lips curled in a near smile, but instead of it making him feel more relaxed that her pain had eased, he felt his own body tensing in response. Maybe he should heed his own words of caution.

"Take a moment and concentrate on taking even breaths. Your lungs will expel the pain, if you give them a chance to do their job," he explained. "Close your eyes and think of the cleansing, healing air moving quietly in and out of your body."

She did as he'd asked, and he watched her face for signs of stress. Instead of paying attention to the little lines of tension around her eyes, though, he found himself watching her long, sable eyelashes softly floating against her freckled cheekbones. He wanted to touch the same place that those lashes touched. Wanted to kiss the tender skin of her lids, the strong jawline—even the jagged scar that marred her features.

Suddenly it wasn't soothing that he wanted. He wanted to bring those features to life with desire…with ecstasy.

He blinked back his growing needs and silently vowed to only consider her needs today. She faced her pain bravely and he needed to help her.

Abby was oblivious to his needs, thank the Powers that Be. Her eyes were closed and her tension lines had eased. The breathing exercises seemed to have done the job.

"Now relax your muscles, Abby. Start with your toes and feet. Feel the tension leaving as you concentrate on letting them go loose."

He watched her visibly begin to relax. Her shoulders eased and her chin dropped slightly.

"Good," he whispered. "Now your knees and thighs. Let them go. They need a rest."

Gray softly slid his arm around her waist. "Now your torso. Keep breathing. My arm will hold you upright, don't worry. Give your muscles a break. Give them a chance to breathe, too."

At last he felt her body slump as the stress of the pain finally worked its way out through her breath and through her pores. "Excellent. Stay relaxed a minute." He gently tightened his grip and eased her loose body off the saddle and into his arms.

But now that he had her there, he realized he didn't want to let her go. She was light as a cloud, soft as the morning mist. He had her pinned against his heart, and that's just where he wanted her to stay.

She tensed in his arms and opened her eyes. He'd apparently waited a moment too long to let her go.

"Gray?"

He eased her down his body and placed her on her feet. "Uh. Keep breathing and relax."

Gray thought that would be good advice to heed himself, if only he could start his heart up again. He hadn't needed a woman in a very long time, and had never desired one the way he did when he was close to Abby. This sudden desperation for her was beginning to be a liability. It was keeping him from doing his duty.

She looked up at him with those sincere green eyes. Her expression was dazed, stunned. Obviously, his passion had stolen into her body. He hadn't meant for that to happen. But apparently they were on the same shaky ground.

"Thanks…for the advice…and the lift off," she heard herself stutter.

What was the matter with her? She'd thought for a moment that he would be kissing her again. That he wanted what her body seemed to be craving. But now he stood there, looking at her so solemnly that she just couldn't be sure. Had she imagined something between them?

Abby knew she didn't have any experience with desire for a man. Hadn't ever thought she would, either. But she was sure that's what had been happening to her.

She wanted the slick feel of his skin against her fingers. Wanted to curl into his arms and have him hold her to his beating heart. Never before had she wanted a man, but she seemed to be frantic for this one.

The thing was, she just couldn't be sure he wanted the same thing she did. She mentally kicked herself for being so green.

"Let's go inside out of the sun." Gray's voice was a little hoarse, but she still wasn't sure what that meant.

He lifted a heavy-looking flap of hide and uncovered a huge archway, leading into the interior of the lodge. Abby peered into the darkness but found that, further inside, light from some source in the roof was illuminating the far corners of the room.

"Kick off your boots," he said as he tugged off his own. "Need any help?"

"I can manage." She pulled them off and left them by the entrance.

She moved under Gray's outstretched arm and strolled inside. The moment she'd crossed the threshold, she felt the change in atmosphere. Trying to remember what he'd told her, she took a deep, sobering breath. She drew the perfume of rawhide, leather and old campfire smoke into her lungs and immediately relaxed.

It felt like home somehow.

As she stood on the soft carpeting of hides, she noted that the one small room felt larger than it really was. But on the other hand, it didn't seem so large that it overwhelmed her. In fact, when she closed her eyes for a second, the impression she got was more like a cozy cradle, softly lulling the muscles of her body into comfort.

As her eyes adjusted to the dim lighting, she saw that Gray had placed a small table and a couple of chairs next to an old stove. In a far corner sat a cot that was literally sagging under the weight of hides and fur. And in another corner an open bookcase held canned goods, water and other necessities.

"The place looks very comfortable," she told him, and meant it.

"It takes care of my needs," he said, sounding slightly proud of himself.

"You built all of this?"

He nodded and indicated that she should sit down at the little table.

"Well, I'm impressed." She eased herself into one of the chairs.

"While I was in college, I spent a couple of summers helping a group of tribal members build houses for some of their poorer neighbors," he said. "This lodge was no trick at all after that. As a matter of fact, I've been thinking of putting in plumbing. I'd be able to get the water from the spring in the woods behind here."

"Speaking of water—" she licked her lips, suddenly thinking how thirsty she'd become "—I could stand a drink."

"Hold on, my little princess. I'll bring you some."

Gray left the lodge, and within a few seconds, returned with the canteen and the bag that held a picnic lunch that Lupe had packed for them. "Guess I forgot that the body also needs food and water in order to heal."

He forgot because his brain had been otherwise occupied with looking at her body, he chided himself. The compact muscles in her thighs and her rounded bottom, gloved snugly in the thick denim of work jeans, had totally wiped away all his good intentions.

She smiled up at him and took a sip from the canteen. After she'd downed a couple of swigs, she handed it back. A few drops of the warm water remained clinging to her lips. Gray gripped the canteen with both hands to keep from reaching over and wiping them away with his thumb.

"Here," he mumbled as he turned away from the ripe vision of her lips. "Let me spread out the sandwiches and fruit we brought with us. Then I'd better go down to the spring and fetch some water. You'd be surprised at how crystal clear and cool the spring water can be."

He saw to it that she took a few bites from the chicken salad sandwich and stayed a minute more to be sure everything was within her reach. When he'd satisfied himself that she was eating and content for the moment, he excused himself, picked up the water bucket and headed to the creek.

Outside in the hazy spring sunshine, he breathed the clear sage-smelling air deep into his lungs, trying to force his head to clear. He needed to find a better way than this to maintain his distance.

She'd given herself over to him for the next few months, letting him take all their safety precautions into his own hands. But he didn't think that would necessarily include actually putting his hands on her body in all the ways he'd been wanting.

Gray made the short pilgrimage to the rocky bank of the little creek. The shade of the tall oaks and the one pecan tree made the journey quite cool and pleasant. Bending to fill the bucket, he decided to bring Abby out here to enjoy the gifts of the Great Spirit on such a magnificent day.

Before he could straighten again, a warm and devious wind struck the back of his neck, lifting the short hairs there and sending a chill down his spine. Someone or something was nearby, and whatever it was didn't belong here with the creatures of the earth.

He set the bucket to the ground gently and crouched low while he stole behind some brush. Sitting perfectly still, Gray searched his surroundings for any sign of what was wrong. Nothing moved except the dappled shadows of sunlight playing tag with the leaves and the wind.

The breeze ruffled his shirt and blew a few fallen

leaves around in the dirt. Suddenly he caught a whiff of something foul and unnatural. Man. There was someone concealed, probably watching the lodge, and perhaps waiting for a chance to make a move.

Gray circled around the trees, training his eyes and ears on any movement. As he moved to the far side of the lodge, the sun came from behind a puffy cloud and glinted off something metallic in a stand of willows nearby.

Keeping low to the ground, Gray made short work of the distance to his quarry. It didn't take much of an effort to find where someone had been hidden, watching the lodge. But that someone was gone.

The spot was some distance away from the lodge, and he figured that what he'd seen shining in the sun's light might've been binoculars. Whoever was there had left in a great hurry.

Gray found horseshoe prints in the soft ground under the willows at the far edge of the stand. None of his mustangs wore shoes, of course, so this had to be a white man's horse.

He raised his head and sniffed the air, hoping to judge which direction they'd headed. Ugh. This was a white man, all right. And one with less than stellar personal hygiene, if the whiff he'd just gotten could be believed.

He followed the horse's prints for a minute, then circled around the lodge and satisfied himself that the intruder had backed off. He wanted to follow the tracks. After all, he couldn't just sit around and wait for someone to attack. But he needed to double-check on Abby first.

Gray picked up the bucket and reentered the lodge. As he stepped inside, he realized that Abby was slumped over the table, still sitting in the chair with her head lying on her folded arms. He didn't have to look twice to know that she'd fallen asleep. She must be worn-out by their ride from the Gentry Ranch.

He threw several furs and hides onto the ground in a cool corner. Then he quietly lifted her from her chair and hoped he could move her to a better position without waking her up.

She stirred and mumbled in his arms, and Gray felt the stirrings of lust as he held her against his chest. Just touching her set off sweet yearnings and riotous wanting.

"Shush, sweetheart. You need your sleep." He laid her down, tucked her within the blankets of fur and stepped back to make sure she was still asleep.

Abby nuzzled against the hides and then fell quiet. The urge to stir her to full awakening by using only his mouth and tongue assaulted his body. His growing need begged him to lie down beside her. But he tossed the needs aside and stepped back out into the midday sunshine.

He had to do something. Abby seemed okay for the moment, but in the long run she was vulnerable. It wasn't in his nature to hide, he was the hunter not the hunted. He went over to speak to Thunder Cloud, who'd been grazing down a slight embankment. "Come and stand guard over her for me, my friend," he pleaded with the mustang. "I will not be so far away that I can't hear if you call."

Thunder Cloud did as he'd asked, moving to stand before the entrance to the lodge. Gray was not worried about her safety from intruders, he would check under every leaf and bush within a hundred yards before he struck out to follow the stalker's tracks. He was much more concerned about keeping her safe from this building lust of his own.

He put on his knee-high moccasin boots, the ones handed down from his grandfather's grandfather, and prepared himself to track the horseman. He hoped he could get a break and find the man stopped somewhere for a rest or a drink.

Gray wanted to unmask the bad guy and end the stalker's quest for Abby. It was just his own nature to defend by going after the trouble. Then he and Abby could go about their business and put an end to this fake engagement.

But he wasn't so sure what he could do to put an end to his own quest for her. Or…where they might end up if he didn't.

Eight

Abby fought, trying to grapple with the crazy images swirling around her. She must've fallen asleep, and this was a dream turned to nightmare. Funny though, even knowing it was a dream, she couldn't manage to wake herself up or shake off the hazy shrouds of billowing smoke.

Gray was here somewhere. She'd seen him for a fleeting second, but now he was gone from view. Searching for him, she began to feel desperate. He was in trouble, she knew it but couldn't do anything for him.

We wish to speak with you, chosen one.

She'd heard the strange, deep voice but couldn't pin down where it was coming from. Panic and plain cold fear grabbed at her throat. But she stiffened and set her jaw.

"Where's Gray? Is he hurt?" she demanded.

The son of our sons needs you, daughter.

The odd voice sounded as if an old Indian brave was speaking to her, but Abby couldn't imagine why he would be calling her daughter. Still…Gray needed her and that was the most important thing. What on earth was happening to her? She shivered and tried to stay calm.

Frustrated and frightened, she cried out, "Where is Gray? I want to help him. Let me go to him."

More sounds, the music of high-pitched flutes and wind chimes magically spilled through the air. A new voice, one that sounded eerily like her grandmother's, spoke to her in hushed tones.

Be still, daughter. He will return to your side in good time. We, the people, have come to warn you and to give you our strength and guidance. A stalker worries you.

"I'm not worried," Abby tentatively interrupted the voice. "Everyone else is worried about me, but I can take care of myself." She might've been scared, but she held her chin high.

The threat is not yours, chosen one. Our son is not aware that a snake is coiled, ready to strike his back.

"Again? If you mean Gray, he's already been bitten by a rattler."

This snake sends all the others. It does not rattle to warn. It strikes by sleuth. Strikes not for protection but for greed.

"You mean that somebody…wants to kill Gray. I'm not the target?" The icy fear moved over her like a shroud.

Our daughter is only in danger by reason of proximity. Do not be fooled.

"Oh my gosh. I have to warn him. Find him."

He will be with you soon. There is one more thing, chosen one.

She needed to find Gray, to tell him what she'd dreamed. Surely this was dream. But she would insist they change the way they'd been going about this business of hiding. Before something terrible happened to him.

She prayed it was not too late.

Listen to your heart, daughter. You will be the mother to our daughters, the renewal of our grand and glorious sons in the ancient grounds. Find your spirit. It will be joined to ours through time. The quest and the vision belong to your heart.

A low drumbeat started, began seeping into her body. It felt like the fog breathed, haunting her, covering her soul with the mist.

Abby panicked—struggled to swim out of its clutches. Gray…she had to find Gray.

Tired, but satisfied that Abby's stalker was long gone, Gray returned to the lodge within twenty minutes and found Thunder Cloud still guarding the entrance. The mustang stood in the long shadows of midafternoon sun, undisturbed and calmly nibbling on some grasses.

"Thank you, old friend. I will take over now," Gray crooned to the mustang.

He'd tracked the intruder's prints as far as he dared on foot and had been surprised to find that, instead of heading toward Gentry Ranch, the horseman had ridden in a straight line toward the Skaggs main house. Gray would have to check later with his stepfather about any strangers who might've been in the area.

Gray barely had a chance to pull off the moccasins when he heard Abby cry out his name. He was at her side before he took his next breath.

She still lay as he left her, cuddled up in the pile of

furs on the floor. But she appeared to be in the throes of a bad dream, flailing her arms and legs and mumbling in her sleep. He knelt beside her, dragging her into his embrace.

"Abby, I'm right here," he soothed her. "Everything is all right. You're in no danger."

She opened her eyes and threw her arms around his neck. "Gray. Thank God. It was so scary…so weird." Breathing into the crook of his neck, she began placing tiny kisses on the sensitive skin there. "I thought I might not be in time to find you."

"In time for what?"

She pulled back to look at him but kept a firm grip around his neck. "To warn you. I had a frightening dream. There were old voices. The voices said it's *you* that's in danger, not me. They said…they said…"

"You had a dream?" he interrupted. "What did you see?"

"It was more like I heard things, not saw them. There were flutes and wind chimes, and I could smell that smoke and heard those drums again. Everything was foggy and filmy."

She was breathing hard, and he could feel her heart hammering in her chest. "Take a breath, Abby. It sounds like you had a vision. You remember when I had a vision. It's nothing to be afraid of. You're okay. Calm down."

"I don't want to calm down," she insisted. "The voices said it's you that someone wants to kill, Gray, not me. You're the one who needs protection."

Abby tightened her grip on his neck and hugged him closer. "An old woman's voice said there was a snake, waiting to strike you again. She meant a person, I know she did. She said someone was greedy, wanting something from you enough to kill you for it.''

Gray could hear the pure panic in her voice, knew from her description that she must've really had a vision. ''But I don't have anything except the mustangs. No one would have a reason to kill me for them, they're not worth enough money.''

''I don't know the reason. The old woman didn't tell me that,'' she complained. ''But I believe what she said. You're the one in danger. You've got to believe me.''

He turned his chin and lightly kissed her ear. ''I believe you, sweetheart. But nothing can happen right this minute. We're safe here for the time being. Thunder Cloud will let us know if we have anything to worry about it.''

Abby sighed against him and he felt her tension ease.

''That's better,'' he murmured. ''Now tell me what else the elder in your vision said.''

Her body tensed against him again. ''Nothing. I've told you everything I can remember.''

Gray clearly heard the lie in her tone, but decided not to push her right now. Perhaps the ancient one in Abby's vision had foretold his death. If that was the case, Gray really didn't want to know.

Instead, he concentrated on Abby. But before he could caution her again to relax, he discovered that his hand was doing its own soothing by diving through the silken tangles of her hair. His fingers rubbed her scalp, gliding through the soft mass of chestnut curls. The satiny sensation was more sensuous than calming.

The air in the lodge changed dramatically. He didn't know when or how or why, but a sudden passion had gripped him in its tender talons.

He kissed her ear again, but this time let his lips linger

to ring the lobe with wetness. Abby uttered a small gasp, and her breathing became shallow, her heart quickened to keep pace with his. He felt her nipples harden against his chest.

"Abby, I want you," he rasped in her ear.

She stayed close, ran her fingertips across his neck, then plowed them through his hair. He heard her sigh.

"I've wanted to touch you for so long," she murmured. "Since the first time I ever laid eyes on you."

The beating of his aroused heart began to drown out all the good reasons why he should not do this. He moaned as his hand moved, almost of its own accord, over the delicate jawline and across her smooth chin.

Gray swallowed hard, feeling every nerve jump to attention. He drew back and watched her slowly open her eyes. The pull of her erotic gaze urged him onward.

A niggling thought in the back of his mind was that Abby would be the last woman he would ever have. Perhaps that thought sprang from a vision of his own impending death. Or perhaps he just wanted her so badly that good sense had deserted him.

He trailed his fingertips lightly over her lips, lost himself in the incredible softness he found there. As if she too were lost, Abby closed her eyes and made a small noise in her throat. The sound sent something shattering and yet awakening through his thickened brain.

Even with her eyes closed, he could see her vulnerability, her desire. She'd tried to hide her nervousness from him, but hadn't realized that by now he knew her too well for that. He was not the hunter with her, but his soul recognized a frightened prey.

Was she afraid of his need? Or of her own?

He prayed silently for guidance, but the red yearning inside him grew unabated. "This should not be," he whispered softly, then swayed toward her. "We will not be together forever. It's not in my vision."

A few whispered words finished him off. "But, Gray, the vision..." she began, then her voice dissolved into a siren's call to passion. "I want you like you said you wanted me."

He bent to kiss her lightly, just a brush across the ripe fullness that drew him. Instantly a light touch seemed beyond him. He grabbed her up and seared her with a deep kiss, both urgent and promising.

Abby responded by making small noises and running her hands over his shoulders and down his arms and chest. He plundered her mouth, kissing and begging for entrance.

She opened, and he thrust his tongue inside to suck and tangle with hers. He marveled at how they seemed to fit together. Lips matched lips. Kisses matched kisses.

He plunged deeply into the desire that was Abby. As he breathed her scent into his body, he smelled deep rich earth and savage, primitive want.

With his heart pounding in his chest, his good sense was lost as his body thickened beyond the bearable. He fought it and pulled back slightly to try one last time.

"We cannot do this, Abby. I have no protection. Think about that. This one time will be all we'll have."

"Gray...please," she said, then smiled, pulling him down to her as she did.

Dizzy, Gray gave up and lost himself in her kisses. If this were to be their one and only time, he would make the most of it. There would be no thoughts of tomorrow or the *nemene* now. There would be only Abby.

While nibbling on her lips, he ran his hands roughly up and down her spine. He felt her shirt bunch under his fingers and tugged it free of her waistband. Before he knew it, his hands were on the tender skin of her back.

Gulping down the pounding urgent need to rush, Gray vowed to take his time. He wanted to experience every bit of this special woman. After all, she'd had her own vision, that made her more magical than ever.

But even before that, he'd thought of her as special. Her strength aroused him. Her gentleness spun him into a much greater web of lust than he'd ever thought possible.

"I must see all of you," he told her in a ragged voice.

She leaned back and smiled again, as if in encouragement. He held her gaze and realized that she wanted to look at him, too. A fierce drumbeat started in his blood, but he forced himself to maintain his patience.

Abby reached for his shirt buttons at the same moment that he began to unbutton hers. A man could endure only so much.

He dragged his shirt from his jeans and ripped it over his head with one quick movement. To hell with buttons.

Her eyes widened. He wasn't sure whether his swift movement had scared her…or if she was admiring his chest.

Either way, he knew he had to slow down when it came to disrobing her.

He reached for the buttons on her shirt once more. When his knuckles grazed the flushed skin at the base of her neck, he felt her tremble with anticipation. He paused and deliberately took a moment's breather.

She placed her hands on his thighs, watching him closely in the dappled afternoon light as it came through the lodge's roof. He remained still while her dark gaze perused him from the tip of his head to his waist. She'd taken her sweet time to study every inch, and when her eyes landed on the scars of his abdomen, he found that his hands were shaking.

Her serious expression suddenly changed into another smile. She shifted and took matters into her own hands. Ripping at her own shirt buttons, she had her arms freed and the cloth pitched away faster than Gray could blink.

The plain white bra she wore didn't do much to hide her swollen nipples from his view. He reached to skim his fingers around the tender skin at the outline of the bra and found his hands steadier.

She shyly lifted her eyes, but gazed directly at him, as if encouraging him to continue. He promised himself once again to take it slowly, make their one and only time last longer than a few minutes.

With slow and deliberately gentle movements, Gray ran his finger up the bra's edge and pushed, first one strap and then the other, off her shoulders. Then he peeled them both down her arms and let the bra pool at her waist.

She dropped her eyelids and flushed. But she remained still and let him get his fill of looking at her. He took in all of her. The firm swell of her breasts, her slim but muscular upper arms, the dusky-rose peaks of her nipples.

"You are so beautiful," he murmured.

She shook her head and made a movement as if to cover herself from his view. "No, I forgot all about the scars. Don't look at me."

Her words stopped the thudding of his pulse as he thought of a better reason to slow things down.

He tenderly grabbed her wrists and held her hands down at her sides. "You are gorgeous. Don't cover yourself from my view. Most of your scars are tiny. Besides, it's not scars that I see when I look at you."

She looked doubtful and hesitant. He wanted that passion back in her eyes.

Gray took one of her hands and placed it against his abdomen. "Look at my scars. Feel them. They aren't ugly, are they?"

She shook her head but kept her eyes trained on his stomach. "They seem to be in some kind of pattern," she said in a raspy voice.

The hoarse, sexy sound reignited the flame of his passion. He gritted his teeth and swore to himself before answering her.

"They are," he muttered. "The red-tailed hawk is my...sort of...good-luck charm. He flies near the sun where I cannot go, and I walk the earth where he dares not tread. We are one within the other."

He took one of her fingers and outlined the featherlike scars spreading out from his belly button. "Here. Feel the beating of his wings through me."

She moaned quietly. But when he dropped his hand, she kept her fingers playing along his sensitive skin. It was soon his turn to moan.

She'd obviously forgotten all about her shyness as she kept watching her own hand trace his scars. So he gave himself permission to drink in the sight of her. He'd really never seen a woman with so much beauty.

The clear, milky-white skin of her breasts gave way to the rosy flush of passion. Just enough of the orange, late-afternoon light shone down on her for him to see all the colors of lust in her body. The longer he watched her, the more her hardened peaks grew bloodred with passion.

His mouth watered at the sight, so he reached for her small rib cage. Quickly moving his hands around to lift her breasts, he bent to take one nipple into his mouth.

When he lapped at the peak, she jerked slightly but then arched to give him better access. And he took full advantage of her move.

He'd originally thought her breasts were small, but now he marveled at how full and rounded they felt in his hands. They fitted his palms perfectly, filled his mouth even better.

As he continued to worship her sensitive bud, she groaned, spurring him into even stronger yearning. He had to make this last. Wanted it to be good for her, too.

He sucked her deeper into his mouth, then pulled back and blew hot breath over her skin. She tasted like honey and wine, he mused. Sweet and tart.

He nipped at her once more. No, he thought, her taste was more like sage and rain. Earthy, salty and sexy.

His fingers replaced his mouth, rubbing and rolling the nubs as his lips moved up her slender neck, making their way back to her mouth. He flicked a nail over one of her peaks and she parted her lips, moaned, then panted with arousal.

Lightly biting those parted lips, he hungrily slipped his tongue between them to feast on more of her tastes. She gripped his shoulders, digging her nails into his skin. His thickened arousal strained against the jeans imprisoning him.

Maddeningly, he fought the last constraints of their clothes. His jeans were gone in an instant and as he tugged at her jeans, she lifted her hips to help.

That one small movement, proving her desire for him, tore past the last of his resolve. He'd been without a woman for too long. The animal in him roared its needs, and his previously tentative patience all but disappeared.

With one hand he grabbed her wrists, lifted them over her head, and pushed her on her back. Gray shoved one thigh hard between her legs and bent to suckle her breasts again.

Moving lower, he nipped the sweet underside of her breast and laved his way down to her navel. Greedily, he tasted, licked, dipped his tongue inside and swirled lower.

His hunger grew. He let go of her wrists and slid his hands down to touch the tips of her nipples. Abby cried out and arched against his palms. He nibbled along the edge of her cotton panties, rejoicing at such a decadent feast.

More. He needed ever more tastes of her. He placed his hand on the heated inside of her sensitive thigh, and at the same time licked slowly down through her panties to the tender spot at the base.

He felt her quiver through the cotton. Tasted the warm wetness spreading over her and heard her cries of pleasure. She drove her hand through his hair, grabbing great handfuls and at the same time tugging at his shoulders, beckoning him to move back up her body.

He did, and she violently kissed his lips, moaning and pleading with everything she had. She writhed and squirmed, sounding as desperate as he felt. Something wild and free had entered their bodies. The sensations were magical, unearthly and beyond any vision.

He tugged at her panties and sat up to drag them down and away from her body. As he shifted to straddle her, he found her eyes watching his jutting sex with fascination.

He stilled, let her drink him in. And then she reached out to touch the sensitive flesh. Tentatively she used her index finger to stroke his tip. It moistened at her touch, and that seemed to both encourage and excite her. She rubbed, slipping down first one side and then the other, causing him to have to bite his tongue to stay still.

The expression on her face was pleasure mixed with amazement. A little niggling thought at the back of his brain warned him to take it easy, that she had never witnessed a man in full arousal before. But his body demanded that he go just a little farther first.

When she dipped a finger back into the slick fountain at his tip, then placed that finger to her mouth and sucked at the taste of him, he lost his last thought entirely.

With a groan he prepared to answer the mating call that swept over both of them. He watched her eyes flash with passion as she raised her hips toward him with a deep moan.

He urgently lifted her buttocks in his hand and positioned himself for a tantalizingly slow slide into the inviting cavern between her legs. She spread her knees wide. He linked hands with her and leaned down on one elbow.

As he slowly entered her wet warmth, a feral groan of pleasure tore from his throat. He hesitated, giving her body time to adjust to his, then moved deeper. She tensed, and he felt a resistance that confused him for only a moment. Then it all made sense.

"You're a virgin," he gasped and fortified himself in preparation to withdraw.

She grasped at his shoulders. "No, please, Gray. Don't back away now. I want you."

He stilled, didn't know which way to turn. Then he looked down into her eyes. Whether it was his imagination or his passion, he could never be sure, but he saw the eyes of Pia, the Great Mother, beckoning him to follow his instincts and his desires.

Abby wrapped her legs around his waist, driving him deeper inside her. She gasped once, then suddenly there was nothing in the world—nothing but heat and tightness and Abby moaning in his ear.

"Please," Abby begged again, as she pulsed with desire.

He knew she pleaded for something that she'd never known. Something he could give her, teach her. The carnal demand became an imperative. It was his honor to show her the pleasures of man and woman.

Pulling her up tightly to his chest and holding her close, he thrust deeply. Her cries turned to sobs, deep and guttural and animalistic. She dug her fingernails into his shoulders, and he lost his way again, forgetting all but the demands of both their bodies.

He bit her shoulder, sucked and tugged at her nipples. The craving turned to insanity. But Abby stayed with him. She arched, straining her neck and pushing her hips upward.

She fought like a wildcat, but it was her own body's resistance that she warred against. She couldn't know how this would end. But he knew.

"Let go, Abby," he gasped. "Let it take you."

He reached between their bodies and flicked his thumb across her swollen nub. Abby arched her back to an impossible angle and screamed. Her body shuddered around him, pulsing with wet, slick pleasure.

Gray picked up the speed of his violent thrusting until he too let go. From somewhere in the distance, he could swear he heard the shriek of the red-tailed hawk. He threw his head back, answering the call with a howl of release.

And all was right with his world. Nothing could touch them now. No power on earth was stronger than what he'd found in Abby's arms this day.

Nine

Gray's body shuddered against her. He collapsed, rolling them both on their sides while keeping Abby tightly entwined in his embrace. Her breathing was ragged and she fought to regulate it like he'd taught her.

But it was no use. There were too many other dazzling thoughts and convulsing tingles quivering around inside her right now. She wanted desperately to stay right here forever, with his slick, sticky skin all warm and cozy surrounding her.

What had just happened? She'd felt drunk, loopy and giddy, spinning on some kind of sensual high. This? This was what making love was all about? Wondering why she hadn't tried it before, she supposed the thought that such an intimate coupling of bodies would be so incredible had simply never entered her mind.

Abby couldn't keep this to herself, she had to share her feelings with Gray. "Wow! That was fantastic." The bubbling, exuberantly girlish giggles left her embarrassed.

At first he said nothing, just bent his head to place a gentle kiss on her hair. He kissed his way to her forehead and then, with a tenderness that was almost heartbreaking, he kissed the scar on her cheek.

"We...I...shouldn't have been that rough. Are you okay?" Gray whispered against her. He lifted up and leaned on one elbow to gaze into her eyes.

Was she okay? She tried to focus, but her body was still pulsing and thumping with sensation. She'd wondered if her aches and pains would be much worse after all she'd done to her body. However, just the opposite was true. Certain parts of her body had gone numb but others simply felt light and energized.

"I'm a little dizzy but, no, nothing hurts," she said with a murmur. "Besides you weren't any rougher than I was."

She lifted her hand and ran a finger around his lips, loving the mere fact that she could do such an intimate thing.

His eyes suddenly changed from soft and unfocused to dark and sensual. The look in those nearly black pools was dangerous, conflicted, as though he were fighting some terrible inner demons. He moved his powerful body against hers and kissed her deeply, drinking her in and draining from her kiss everything he seemed to be seeking.

He arched his hips aggressively and Abby realized that their bodies were still connected. And on top of that, Gray was apparently not finished with showing her about lovemaking. She felt the burgeoning thrust of pleasure as it sent rippling currents throughout her body again.

"I've gone mad with wanting you," he groaned. "I

know this is wrong. You'll be in pain later.'' He gasped when she pushed her hips against his groin.

''Abby, we're not protected,'' he moaned through gritted teeth. ''And I still can't make a commitment to you. This should not happen again.''

The power overtook her. And what she wanted was more.

That's what this feeling was, she'd decided. A woman's power to make a man do what she wanted. Abby placed her lips against his chest and licked her way down to his nipples. He grew thicker inside her and shuddered against her belly.

This time they moved in slow motion. He kept their bodies joined together as they lay on their sides. Drawing in and out from her in a tantalizing way, he teased until she begged.

Then he reached a hand to pluck at her nipple, bending his head to suck on her neck. She heard herself panting, crying, sobbing out words that made no sense.

Gray's breath came in shallow pants, as well. The flushed sensation spread across her body again, and she knew she was close to spinning off the edge of the world.

Just as the thunder began to ring in her ears, he withdrew. She gasped but he quickly positioned himself at the crease between her hip and thigh. Placing two fingers deep inside her, he flicked his thumb over her most sensitive spot. They convulsed together as their ecstatic cries mingled in the silence of the late afternoon. Abby's world tilted when the climax rocked through her body, and she felt Gray pump his seed onto their pallet of hides.

Finally her trembling subsided, and they lay sated and sweaty, wrapped in each other's arms. When all her senses returned, Abby rolled slightly, to find more breathing room. The cold, wet spot she brushed her bottom against reminded her of what Gray had done.

She touched his forehead and stroked his cheek, making lazy circles with her fingers. ''Are you all right?'' she breathed in a hoarse rasp.

He smiled at her, and she felt her heart leap. ''I'm more than okay,'' he said and kissed her lightly on the tip of the nose.

Gray's hand wandered down her neck, across her breasts and down her arm. ''You aren't at all as slender as I thought,'' he said quietly. ''Your muscles are firm, sexy…magnificent.'' He ran his fingers down her thigh, learning her body and making her skin ripple in response.

''And you—'' she blushed and stammered ''—you're more than I…bigger than I would've…'' Lying here naked, after all they'd done together, she still felt herself turning the colors of a soft sunset.

His eyes gleamed in appreciation, then turned serious once more. ''Abby,'' he began. ''Why didn't you tell me?''

''What? Oh, you mean about being a virgin?'' She shrugged it off. ''It wasn't important. Besides, I really had no intention of…doing what we just did. I didn't know—'' She hesitated, tried to remember to breath. ''Is it always that spectacular?'' she asked, with the wonder of it still cracking her voice.

His expression grew tight, hard. ''No…no, it's never been that way before for me.''

Suddenly he was withdrawing from her emotionally. She could feel it. Dang. She didn't want this to end so soon.

He rolled away and sat up on their makeshift pallet

on the floor. ''Abby. Listen to me. I shouldn't have done this. But I lost myself in you. That's not sensible, especially for a man with other commitments and pledges to keep.''

''What commitments? Are you engaged to someone else or something and haven't bothered to tell me?''

He shook his head, the look in his eyes turned downright grave. ''Not yet. But I am committed to the *nemene.* When I marry, it will be to a woman that is chosen by the elders for me.'' He turned his head, looked away for a minute. ''I know that the woman I marry must have the blood of my ancestors to bring sons to the tribe. It is our way.''

The anger flared in her with swift sharp barbs of spite. ''Yeah? Well, who wanted you to make a commitment, anyway?'' She knew she sounded childish but she couldn't seem to help herself. ''All I ever asked for was a *pretend* engagement.''

She crawled away from him and got to her feet, looking for her clothes. ''I was only joking about it being so great. I didn't really mean it. And except for keeping the neighbor boys off my back, I would never have considered being engaged to someone like you.''

He moved quickly, grabbed her by the shoulders. ''I'm not good enough for the heiress of Gentry Ranch, is that it?'' His eyes were hard now, black and blinded with temper.

She'd sucked in a shocked breath at his fury. ''No,'' she huffed. ''Don't be ridiculous, that's not it. That's not what I meant at all.'' His anger had somehow dissipated hers. ''I just meant that we could never work things out, since you don't want to stay in Castillo County. While I, on the other hand, can't think of anyplace else I'd rather be.''

Her shoulders slumped and she realized his hands were still gripping her. "Let go of me," she said calmly.

Gray looked down at his large hands and jerked them away from her like a flame too hot to touch. "I didn't mean to hurt you. I never meant to hurt you," he said softly.

"You didn't," she lied. "I'm fine."

She pulled up her bra, which she'd suddenly realized was still around her waist. Then she scooped up her shirt, jabbed her arms into the sleeves and began to button.

"We have to talk about where we go from here," he said carefully. "There's still our fake engagement and a stalker out there who doesn't seem to care too much whether you get in his way or not."

Abby felt bruised. Not in the physical sense, of course. Although she did have a few new aches in places that had never hurt before. But her spirit was battered and it confused her. The only thing she seemed to have left was a little pride.

"I have my commitments, too, you know," she said dryly. "Our deal is not all one-sided. The elders in my vision said I was to warn you and watch out for you." She pulled on her jeans and looked around for her boots. "I intend to do my duty and save your high-and-mighty tribal rear end. I'm sticking with you, Gray. Like we said. There's nothing you can do to shake me loose."

He reached out to steady her, laid one hand lightly on her shoulder. "Yes. We will finish our charade. Now that we know the truth, we'll find out who's been doing this."

Letting his hand drop back to his side, Gray turned sadly and retrieved her boots. "Here," he said, handing them to her. "And Abby…" His voice sounded so tentative, so unlike Gray, that she wondered what he wanted to tell her.

"I still owe you my life. That will never change. I'll stick by you, have no fear of that. But we must not repeat our actions of today. We should maintain a friendship and protect each other, nothing more."

Yeah, she thought. Anything else was too danged hard. "I agree, Gray. Nothing more." They dressed in silence.

Riding toward the Gentry Ranch, just as the first evening star twinkled in the heavens, Abby thought about her promise to stand by Gray. He'd saved her life and had agreed to her silly charade. She knew she owed him and decided to do everything in her power to keep him safe.

She made tons of promises to herself, as well. She vowed not to lose her senses ever again when he was near. She was done with that, she hoped. And when he left, she would not look back. She'd go on with her life and become the best danged ranch foreman that ever existed.

She rather neatly buried the rest of her weird vision, too. She pushed deep into her heart the part she'd failed to mention to Gray. Those elders must've been mistaken in their predictions about her being the mother to their sons. It was clear she wasn't the chosen one. At least, not as far as Gray was concerned.

"You want to run the part about a 'vision' by me one more time?" Cinco asked the question with disbelief in his voice. He leaned back in his huge, leather chair and waited.

Gray had known this would be difficult. He'd worried about it all night while trying to sleep on the couch in the Gentrys' great room. Explaining his beliefs to a white man who didn't have an open mind seemed rather fruitless, but Abby had insisted that they try with her brother. Gray set his jaw and folded his arms over his chest.

"I'm trying to, if you'll please listen," Abby pleaded.

She began to pace back and forth in front of Cinco's desk while she flung her fisted hands in the air, punctuating her points. Gray leaned against the wall of Cinco's office, amusing himself by watching her while he waited to see what her brother's response to her interpretations would be.

Abby replayed both of their visions—and Gray's grandfather's explanations as well. She did a fine job, but Gray still had to wonder what it was that she'd been told in her vision that she continued to leave out.

When she finally wound down, Cinco turned to him. "Okay, Parker. Let's say for the moment that I buy this vision thing. What do you have that someone would want badly enough to kill you for? Not the mustangs, I know better."

Gray straightened up and shrugged a shoulder. "Beats me. But I do know that yesterday afternoon someone was watching us while we were at my lodge on Skaggs property."

Abby swiveled her head hard to stare at him. Her eyes shot little daggers of dark meaning and he guessed he should have told her about the stalker first. But she didn't make any remarks about what he'd said to Cinco.

"Tell me a little about how you came to own the mustangs," Cinco calmly inquired as he steepled his fingers in front of his face.

Gray told him the best he could about his mother's will and his stepfather's response to it. The legal proceedings had been mercifully short. Gray didn't understand wills and trust and such, but fortunately the judge had dismissed Joe Skaggs's claims almost as fast as he'd brought them up.

"Hmm," Cinco murmured, when Gray finally finished with all he could remember. "Mind if I do a little checking around? I'd like to dig into your stepfather's business a bit, and I have a friend at the county courthouse who might be able to shed some light on the subject. Lawsuits are public proceedings in this county."

Gray shrugged. "Be my guest, if you think it'll help."

"Knowledge is always powerful," Cinco told him. "The more information we have, the easier it will be to dig out a motive for what's been happening."

Cinco pushed back his chair and stood. "In the meantime," he began, addressing both his sister and Gray. "Just to be on the safe side, I think you should change the way you've been going about things."

Abby jumped in front of her brother with a scowl on her face. "If you're about to suggest that we split up, don't bother, bubba. We're sticking together and that's all there is to it."

Cinco grinned down at her, then lifted his eyes to include Gray. "I wouldn't think of splitting you up, sugar," he drawled. "But I do think it's odd that all your troubles have been occurring at or near the Gentry-Skaggs fence line."

Gray imagined that fact had just proved their point. "You're saying you believe the threat is really mine?"

"Well, it's a definite possibility. One we can't afford to ignore." Cinco laid a hand on Abby's shoulder. "Why don't you two try staying as far removed from the border between our two ranches as possible?"

He turned to Gray. "In fact, I think it'd be a good

idea for you to stay off Skaggs land entirely for a while.''

''I can't. I have a responsibility to the mustangs.''

Cinco shook his head. ''You could teach one of the Gentry Ranch wranglers what to do. Why don't you call your stepfather and tell him you and Abby are going away for a few days and that she'll be sending a hand over to feed and check on the mustangs.''

Gray started to object. He didn't know if he could trust someone else with the care of his herd. But then he glanced over at Abby. At the angry red scar on her cheek and the vulnerable look in her eyes. And let duty make his decision.

''Yes, I'm sure my stepfather would allow that. But I'll need to pick up a few things.''

Cinco nodded. ''Right. Leave Abby here at the house and take Jake Gomez with you to watch your back. Do you have to enter the Skaggs main house to get what you need?''

''Hold on just a minute, bubba,'' Abby interjected. ''Why do I have to stay here?''

''I don't want you anywhere near Skaggs property until this whole thing blows over,'' Cinco told her. ''I'm sure Gray understands what I mean.''

Gray reached toward Abby and took her hand into his, giving her strength through his touch. ''Your brother is right, Abby. I can go quicker and easier if I don't have to worry about you being hurt because of me.'' He didn't drop her hand but turned to address Cinco. ''I don't have to go anywhere near their main house to pick up my things. Most of what I need will be at my lodge.''

''But, Gray…'' Abby broke in.

He turned his attention back to her. ''I won't be gone long. A couple of hours at most.''

"Yeah," Cinco broke in. "And you'll be real busy getting a few of your things together, too, missy."

"Me?" she asked. "Where am I going?"

"I think it might be very clever if you two really put on a show of going away," Cinco urged. "That way, anyone who would be a danger to you from either the Skaggs *or* the Gentry ranches will let their guard down until you return. We should get the break we need before then."

"But where'll we go?" Abby inquired with a grumble. "I don't want to leave the Gentry."

Cinco chuckled and shook his head slightly. "No, sugar, I know you wouldn't let some potentially dangerous threat push you off your beloved ranch. But I've had another thought. You remember Granddad Teddy's little cabin down by Rockridge Creek?"

Gray watched Abby's eyes light up with something very different than he'd ever seen there. Something soft maybe. Or *wistful* might be a better word, he couldn't be sure.

"Of course I do," she told her brother. "We played there day after day when we were little. How could I forget that. I love that cabin."

Cinco inclined his head. "Well, Meredith and I were down that way a few weeks ago. The cabin needs some work, but the roof is sound and the well is still pretty decent." He flicked a glance over to Gray. "If I take a truck with supplies, some tools and a generator, can you make the place livable for a week or two?"

"Sure. I suppose so." Gray thought about the possibility of spending a couple of weeks alone with Abby and very nearly told Cinco his idea stunk. How would he ever be able to keep his hands off her under those circumstances? Especially now that he knew what treasures awaited him.

"But, uh, how many rooms does this cabin have?" he asked her brother.

Cinco laughed and put a hand on Gray's shoulder. "Why? You worried that Abby's friends and relatives will think poorly of her for spending a week alone with you?" He punched Gray's arm. "No one will know where you two are except Meredith and me and Jake. And we're not overly concerned about our engaged sister sleeping in a cabin with her fiancé."

Gray felt a constriction in his chest at the thought of lying to Cinco. Gentry was a man who'd always treated him honorably. He was the first white man Gray had ever trusted implicitly, and Abby loved him without reservations.

In addition to the lie about the engagement, Gray didn't want to think about staying night after night in the same one room with Abby, the woman he was trying desperately to keep at a decent distance. He decided he didn't care much for either of these looming circumstances.

"Okay. Look, Cinco," he began. "I think we'd better tell you..." Gray hesitated as Abby tightened her grip on the hand she still held, squeezing down with a fierce grasp.

She caught Gray's gaze with a sharp and pointed stare. Her meaning was quite clear.

"Tell me what?" Cinco prodded.

Gray shook his head and backed off. "Oh, never mind," he saw the relief flood into Abby's eyes. "It's just that I've had some experience in remodeling houses, and you might not like everything I will do to this little cabin of yours."

That brought a smile to Cinco's suddenly serious face. "Oh, don't you worry about that any. You go right ahead and improve whatever you want," he said through a wide grin. "I suspect my sister will keep you way too busy to get much remodeling done, though."

And that, Gray muttered to himself, was exactly what he was afraid of.

Abby was still mumbling cuss words under her breath twenty minutes later as she jammed a few more pairs of jeans into a soft duffel bag. Her mind was reeling with questions and goofy emotions she wished would go away. There was nothing she hated worse than all this confusion and turmoil.

If Cinco hadn't suggested that she and Gray go to the Rockridge Creek house, she might've confessed the truth right then and stayed here at the main house far away from the confusing temptation that Gray presented. But the little cabin from her childhood drew her.

Actually, she'd been sorely missing the cabin ever since her parents' disappearance. But she hadn't had the nerve to face the place alone. The rough-sawn rooms and quaint stone fireplaces reminded her too much of her mother. Abby tried to think why that was. She shrugged and decided it must've been because her mother had always been so fond of the place.

Abby's mother's family had been Texans for even longer than the Gentrys—nearly two hundred years now, and Kay Gentry had treasured her roots. Mom always said the cabin reminded her of the stories she'd been told of the early settlers and the hardships they'd endured to make a home.

Abby blinked and found wetness on her cheeks. Drat. Maybe going to the Rockridge cabin was not such a terrific idea. Not only would she be faced with having to deal with what she felt about Gray, but she might also have to deal with the buried memories of her mother.

Kay Gentry's memory was something Abby needed to keep folded gently away inside her heart. No one could help her with it, no one could bring her mother back.

But the problem of Gray and the things he made her feel, that was something she had to talk to someone about. Someone who had a little more experience with this kind of thing.

She zipped up the bag and tugged it down the stairs in search of her sister-in-law. Meredith was someone she could ask without being too embarrassed. After all, Meredith was married to Cinco now and would at least understand why she needed to know.

Abby found her sister-in-law in the office that Cinco had made especially for her. Here Meredith kept flight plans, maps, books and two computers. But it wasn't a sterile, dry workroom. No, the walls were painted in a soft, sage green, the couch covered in butter-colored leather and the polished wood floor gleamed with a feminine shine.

Cinco had put Meredith in charge of the ranch's fleet of aircraft. She flew the corporate jet when necessary, did her turn as one of the range pilots and scheduled all the other flights that flew in and out of the Gentry Ranch airstrip.

She was a fantastic pilot, Abby knew, but Meredith was also approachable and understanding. The two of them had shared a special bond since almost the moment they'd met.

Meredith loved Cinco with a passion that showed clearly in her eyes, and Abby loved her for that, too.

"Hey, you got a minute?" she asked after she knocked softly on Meredith's open door.

"Abby Jo." Meredith moved toward her, grabbing her up in a huge hug. "How're you feeling, sweetie? I've been so worried about you."

"Well...physically I'm fine, but..." She hesitated, not really knowing how to begin.

"Ah. You've got heart troubles, is that it?" Meredith dragged her into the room. "Come on in, have a seat and we can at least talk them out."

Meredith offered her a glass of water. "I've been meaning to talk to you about Gray, anyway."

Abby absently accepted an icy bottle and set it down on the old stage-coach chest Meredith was using as a side table. "Oh? What do you want to know about Gray?"

"I guess maybe it's not really Gray I want to know about," Meredith began. "But I've been doing some research on Texas history...as a surprise for Cinco. You see, I figure if I'm going to be a Texas rancher, I should know what's happened to the land and the people in the past."

Abby took a swig from the water bottle and nodded. That sounded like something her very thorough and precise sister-in-law would tackle.

"Anyway..." Meredith opened a bottle for herself and took a swallow. "I've come across the name Parker a couple of times and I was just wondering if maybe Gray is related to them...even though he doesn't claim Texas as his home."

"Parker?" Abby searched her brain for that name in her state's history.

"I recently finished reading the story of Cynthia Anne Parker who was captured in a raid and was raised by the

Comanche,'' Meredith explained. ''The name and the fact that the Indians were Comanche sort of rang a bell with me. Do you know anything about it?''

''Sure, I do. Everybody knows that sad story. Most of us 'round this part of Texas have Comanche blood in our backgrounds, but that story makes us want to keep it quiet. I don't have any idea if Gray is related to that Parker.''

''You and Cinco are part American Indian?''

Abby nodded. ''A little. Way, way back.''

''Tell me your version of the Parker story will you?'' Meredith asked. ''It's always better to hear from a native.''

''Okay.'' Abby brought the old story back to the forefront of her mind. ''It was 1836 and Texas was barely settled. Mexico still claimed most of the land, but that was the year we won our independence. The Comanche were trying to keep the range open so the buffalo herds and wild horses would have room to roam. Anglos that came from the east to settle here faced dangers from several fronts.

''Cynthia Anne Parker was nine years old when she was captured by a Comanche raiding party,'' Abby continued. ''Instead of killing children during those times, the Indians generally took them and raised them as their own. Most of the kids were never found or heard from again.''

Abby took another swig of water and could clearly hear her grandmother's voice retelling the wretched tale of the kidnapped little girl. ''Anyway...when Cynthia Anne was about thirty-three the Texas Rangers found her with her new Comanche family. They recaptured her and killed her Indian husband, but her children managed to run away and escaped back to their tribe.

"But Cynthia Anne had been Comanche for too long." Abby shook her head sadly. "She didn't want to come back to her white roots. But her Texan relatives refused to let her go home to her children. She pined away, couldn't accept the strange white man's ways that she'd forgotten.

"In less than four years poor lost Cynthia Anne died of a broken heart."

"What happened to her children?" Meredith asked quietly.

Abby thought a minute. "I'm not sure about them all, but I do know that one of her sons grew up to be a very famous chief, Quanah Parker." She smiled at the memory of his story. "He lived a long time and married many women. Had over twenty children I've heard tell."

"So Gray might be related to him?" Meredith probed.

"Maybe," Abby murmured. "I'll ask him." Something in the story she'd just told was important, she mused. But for the life of her she couldn't think of what it was she'd said or why it would be of any consequence.

Abby dragged her thoughts back to the present and decided she'd better get to why she'd sought out Meredith in the first place. "I was just wondering if you could tell me a little about…how to make a man, uh, want to make love."

Abby clapped her hand over her mouth the minute the words were out. She couldn't believe she'd had enough guts—or was that stupidity—to ask such a question.

After a momentary surprised look, Meredith's whole face wrinkled up in a mirth-filled smile. "Oh? Haven't you two—you know—done the deed yet?"

Oh, God. This had been truly a stupid move. "Of course we have," Abby quickly clarified. "It's nothing like that. He just… Well, the truth is, he said he doesn't want to do it again.'' She hesitated and remembered to keep up the pretense of their story. ''Until we're married that is. Do you think that's because he didn't like what we did?''

''Oh, I doubt that. But you liked it too well to wait?'' Meredith guessed.

''Yeah,'' Abby sighed. That was the real truth. Even though she didn't want a long-term commitment any more than he did, she'd realized she did want to be close to Gray again. She needed to find out more about the strange feelings she had when they were lying in each other's embrace.

Meredith threw an arm around her shoulders. ''Well, I know a couple of things that might help.'' She grinned. ''But first, show me the clothes that you've packed to take with you to the cabin.''

''Clothes? You mean like jeans and shirts?''

''No, sweetie,'' Meredith purred. ''I mean like underwear and nightgowns.''

Ten

"Abby, please talk to me." Gray thought the silence had gone on long enough.

Cinco and Jake Gomez had just left with their trucks and trailers, and Abby was busying herself with carting supplies into the cabin. On their entire long ride over here on the backs of Thunder Cloud and Abby's mare, she'd said no more than a few words.

Gray had tried to get her to tell him what she was thinking, whether she was angry at him for almost revealing their secret to her brother. But she'd simply shaken her head and stayed quiet. He didn't want to make her any madder—but enough was enough.

"What is going on in that pretty head of yours?" he tried again.

"We'll have lots of time to talk later," she glared at him. "Right now I want to get this gear stowed and then see about making a lean-to for the horses."

Ever practical, that was his Abby.

The minute he'd thought the words he tried to squelch them. But it was too late. He did think of her as his. At least, he wished for it to be so.

She was so beautiful, so full of life. The woman was the most earthy, erotic creature he'd ever beheld. And yet, she could dream, see visions, be a real treasure when need be. He wanted badly to touch her, to hold her in his arms once again.

The need rose up and choked him. It was so much more than want. He simply had to possess her, fill himself up on the essence of Abby.

"You going to stand around day-dreaming all day? Or do you want to show me all this grand handiwork you've been bragging about?" she urged dryly.

Right, he thought, swallowing hard. He had to get his head out of the clouds and back to reality. She was never going to be his. He couldn't even touch her again, that wouldn't be honorable.

It was a good thing the dusk came so late at this time of year. A long day was about to become even longer.

Gray finished hooking up the generator that Cinco and Jake set up. The cabin appeared to have been wired a generation or so ago, for what purpose Gray wasn't entirely sure because he didn't think the place had been inhabited for more than fifty years. But it did have lights and a couple of small appliances. A refrigerator and a water heater were the best of the bunch.

However, the plumbing was not in the best shape. A trickle of hot water to wash up with was better than none at all, he guessed. Gray could see he had his work cut out for him in trying to make this place more livable.

He stepped back outside and found that Abby had unsaddled her horse and unloaded the pack animals they'd trailed along. Gray was amazed to see her currying Thunder Cloud—and the mustang was standing still for her attentions, too.

Gray had to hold back a chuckle. Looked as if Abby had managed to charm more than just one lone Comanche.

"Come sit a minute and have something cool to drink," he urged.

She looked up at him, but her eyes were hidden by the shadow from the brim of her work hat. "We need to make a shelter for the horses, something to give them a little shade from the hot sun. We'll take a break when we're done."

"Abby, these horses will be fine for a night or two without a shelter. You know that as well as I do. It's spring…not the middle of a sweltering summer…nor the dead of winter. Thunder Cloud spends most of his time on the range, anyway. If you're so worried about shade, we can tether them down under the willows by the creek."

"But…" she fumed. "Oh, all right. If you'll bring out the food and drinks Lupe packed for us, I'll take a break. I just want to give the horses a little feed first."

"Abby. You'll spoil these animals. There's plenty of grass around here." He grinned. She was splendid, caring more for the horses than for herself. But he wasn't going to mention to her now how he felt. It was all he could do to keep his distance and talk in a coherent manner around her.

She ignored him and went to open the feed packs. Gray retrieved the cold fried chicken and the thermos filled with lemonade. If she didn't want to leave the horses, he'd set up a little picnic for the two of them outside.

He dragged the old, rough-sawn table out of the kitchen and set it up outside. Every time he moved to where he could catch a glimpse of her, he marveled at how Abby just seemed to fit here, taking care of the horses and using the muscles in her body the way the Great Spirit had intended.

When he was finally ready, he cajoled her into joining him for a break. Now that the two of them were seated on the benches, he hoped to find a way of getting her to talk more about what was going on inside her head.

Abby surprised him by asking a question first. "By any chance, are you related to Chief Quanah Parker?" she mumbled past her first bite of chicken.

"What a question." He smiled at her, though, thrilled that she might be interested in his background. "But yes, Quanah Parker, son of the chief of the Noconi, was one of my ancestors. As a boy, I remember my grandfather taking me to see his gravesite at Ft. Sill, Oklahoma. The granite marker and his statue made quite an impression on me. I'll never forget the words chiseled on that monument."

Gray hesitated, but Abby seemed quite interested, so he quoted the first part for her. "'I am a thousand winds that blow. I am the diamond glint in snow. I am the sunlight on ripened grain. I am the gentle autumn rain.

"'When you wake in the morning hush, I am the swift uplifting rush…of quiet birds in circling flight. I am the soft starlight at night.'"

"It's wonderful," Abby sighed. "I didn't know you had the soul of a poet…I mean…that you would care to remember words of such great beauty."

Gray grinned at her and swallowed a last bite of potato salad. "I'm quite a connoisseur of great beauty wherever I find it." He reached to wipe a stray crumb from her chin, leaving his fingers there to caress the soft skin around her mouth and over her lips. "I see great beauty in you, Abby."

Her eyes widened, but she pulled back away from his touch. "I'm not even pretty, let alone beautiful," she mumbled. "But I think you qualify as gorgeous...handsome."

"Ah. I see we have a mutual admiration for each other," Gray said. "That's good. At least, we won't have to look at ugliness while we spend the next few days together."

Abby squirmed in her seat and started to fiddle with the paper plates on the table. "We'd best clean up here, if you're done." Her expression seemed flustered and bothered. It was charming.

"Right," he chuckled. "The evening star is out and it will soon be too dark to work outside. It's time to find a spot inside where we can lay out the bedrolls for the night."

A flash of terror moved across her eyes before she stood and turned away from him. "I think I'd rather sleep outdoors. I'll set up a place down by the creek with the horses. You suit yourself."

He was up and had a hand on her shoulder before he could think it through. "Abby, wait a minute. You're not afraid of me, are you? You said you weren't before."

She shook her head, but he saw a sheen of tears appear in her eyes.

"Sit down and talk to me about this for a second."

She hesitated but reluctantly sat back down on the table's bench.

Gray sat beside her. "You remember I said that what happened between us must not happen again, don't you?'' He didn't wait for her nod. ''I meant every word of that, Abby. You have nothing to fear from me.''

Her eyes grew wide then sad. ''No, it isn't that,'' she said. ''In fact, I'd really like to...''

She stopped, drawing in a cleansing breath. ''It isn't you I'm afraid of, Gray. In fact, I would like it very much if you'd come lie beside me again.''

''Then what are you afraid of?'' he asked softly. Whatever it was, Gray wanted to fight it off for her. He wanted to take that look from her eyes.

She twisted and looked at the cabin. ''Memories,'' she replied wistfully. ''I just can't seem to make myself stay inside the cabin for very long. It hurts me...deep inside somewhere...it really hurts me.''

''But I thought you loved this old place. Didn't you say that?''

''Yes, I did.'' She blinked her eyes as though in pain. ''But that was before I stepped inside and looked around. I can't...I can't seem to make myself go back again.''

''Tell me what you saw there that upset you so,'' he inquired warily. ''Maybe I can change it for you...make it easier for you to take.''

She shook her head, but gently smiled up at him. ''There isn't anything you can do. It's just the ghosts that I see, and you can't make them go away.''

Abby fought to put her feelings into words. Gray seemed so sincere in wanting to help. She knew he couldn't fix this problem for her, but he did deserve an explanation.

''I can hear my mother's voice in the cabin, telling me about her Texas ancestors and how we were going to fix the place up...make it a real home for one of us kids,'' she began slowly. ''Mom always loved this place, she'd played here as a little girl. And when she got married, Daddy fixed the cabin up enough so they could spend their honeymoon here.''

Abby felt the burn of tears and scrunched up her eyes to hold them off. ''My brother Cal and I spent hours playing in these old rooms. Cinco came along for a while, but he was older and soon found girls were a lot more fun than a younger brother and sister.'' She shrugged a shoulder. ''Cal and I made up stories and acted them out. We became stars, cowboys and plains settlers like our ancestors.''

Gray reached for her hands, obviously wanting to soothe by giving her the warmth of his touch.

She shook her head and quietly fisted her hands so she could continue without breaking down. ''The last time I ever saw my mother she told me she was going to fix up this old place for me…'like a little dollhouse' she said. Cal was about to follow Cinco off to college so I wanted a place to go off to, as well. Mom said as soon as she and Dad got back from this cruise they were going to take, that we'd get started here.''

Abby bit down hard on her lip and fought the images. ''She didn't keep that promise. She never came home. I…well, I decided I didn't need any old dollhouse. Just like I didn't want anybody's old promises, either. Anyway, I'm the kind of person who'd rather be outside with the horses and working on the ranch.''

''Abby.'' Gray slid his arm around her shoulder and squeezed her to him. ''You don't have to face your ghosts if you don't want to. I'll set up camp outside with you. We'll work mostly on the plumbing, roofing and painting. If there's any work to do inside, I can do it alone.''

''Really? You don't mind setting up camp outside?'' She couldn't believe he was so tenderhearted and gentle.

His caring words almost caused the dam to break in her resolve not to cry.

"Now what kind of Comanche would I be if I had to spend all my time indoors?" he joked. "We'll just pretend like we're on an old trail ride. Only instead of herding cows, we'll be rounding up a remodeled cabin. Okay?"

Forty-eight hours later, Abby wiped the sweat from the back of her neck with a grimy bandanna and silently cursed the hot spring sun. There were a couple of things about constantly living and working out-of-doors that didn't seem so romantic when you were standing knee deep in them, she mused. Not having a hot shower or a washing machine were two things she missed most of all.

She straightened her back to loosen the kinks and looked around for Gray. He'd climbed down the ladder a few minutes ago, saying he needed a couple more handfuls of shingles.

Speaking of Gray, that was the other thing she would change if she could—having another chance with him. Sleeping in bedrolls by a campfire might be fine for a trail rider or a Girl Scout, but it was sure leaving her empty-handed in the man-teasing department.

She dreamed about sneaking into his bedroll in the middle of the night. Longed to have his hands touching her in all the sensitive places again. But Gray kept his distance, shook his head when she began to beg and told her he had not forgotten his promises. Meanwhile all that fancy underwear that Meredith had rushed her out to buy was still brand-spanking new…unused and waiting to be unpacked.

Gray's bodiless and tentative shout, coming from the

ground, startled her, making her scan the horizon to see what might be wrong. ''Abby, I think you'd better come down off the roof right away.''

She saw it then, the cloud of dust, moving across the prairie and heading in their direction. Someone was on the dirt road, leading to the cabin.

Scrambling off the roof and down the ladder, Abby raced to her packs and pulled out her cell phone. She flipped it open, punching in Cinco's number code as she did.

Nothing happened. She pulled the phone from her ear and starred at a blank digital screen.

''The phone's dead,'' she told Gray.

''Not surprising. You have to plug them in to an electric current occasionally to charge them up, don't you?'' he inquired dryly.

She shot him what she hoped was a ''ha-ha, very funny'' look. ''We brought binoculars. Let's see if we can find them in the packs somewhere.''

Gray found the binoculars and adjusted them for the distance to the oncoming cloud. ''Looks like your brother's trucks.''

Abby picked up her rifle and checked the load.

Ten minutes later Cinco stepped down from the cab of the first pickup. Meredith drove her pickup right in beside his and turned off the motor.

''I hope you don't mean to use that on us, baby sister,'' Cinco laughed and nodded toward the rifle still in her hand.

She put the gun down and shook her head at her ignorant but endearing brother. ''You damn near got blown off the face of the earth, bubba. Why didn't you let us know you were coming out here?''

Meredith moved to grab Abby up in a giant hug. ''We

tried calling you, but we didn't get an answer. We have some good news to share.''

Abby watched her suspicious brother take in the situation with one sweeping glance around the place. It was quite obvious that she and Gray had not moved inside the cabin. She wondered what Cinco would have to say about that.

Gray stepped to her side, as if he wanted to defend her somehow from any possible accusations Cinco might make. But her brother just grinned at him and reached to shake his hand and pat him on the back.

''How're things going?'' Cinco smiled and waved an arm toward the trucks. ''We've brought another load of supplies for you two...along with a couple of pieces of information.''

''Let's sit down at the table,'' Meredith added. ''I'll unload the ice and cold drinks we brought. I can't wait to tell you what's happened, Abby.''

Within minutes the table had been swept clear of the tools and sawdust that had littered the top, and everyone was seated with a cold drink in their hands. Abby was a little nervous. She wasn't entirely sure about this turn of events.

''Abby,'' Cinco began. ''Congratulations. You're an auntie.''

The shock of his words left her mouth open. This was not what she thought she would hear. In fact, she'd totally forgotten that her brother Cal had been expecting a child.

''A baby girl,'' Meredith chimed in. ''She's a sweet little thing. We saw a digital picture from the hospital's computer-cam.''

Cal had not been terribly thrilled about having this baby, Abby knew. In fact, he'd refused to allow any of the family to come to his and Jasmine's quickie wedding a few months ago. Thinking of the tiny brand-new Gentry, Abby hoped her brother's attitude would now soften.

"When can we see her?" she asked.

"Jasmine has asked us to wait until they bring her home from the hospital." Meredith fairly bubbled with excitement. "But that's tomorrow. The hospitals kick them out after a couple of days, I understand."

Abby smiled at her dear sister-in-law. She knew Meredith had never had any family and this new baby was going to go a long way toward making her feel like the Gentry family was becoming her own.

"Cal's named her Kaydie Elizabeth," Cinco said in a hushed tone.

Abby felt the cold fingers of grief reach inside her and clutch at her heart. "After Mom and Grandma?" she whispered.

Cinco nodded solemnly. "I'm hoping that's a sign that Cal is ready to begin accepting everything in his life and will start settling down."

Abby wanted to agree with her brother. Wanted to be able to talk about the family in an adult manner. But she couldn't just now. The sky had suddenly turned from bright cobalt blue to deepest charcoal, and the humidity was oppressive, closing in around her.

She felt something squeeze her hand—hard. Turning, she realized that Gray was by her side and she looked up into his face. He mouthed the word *breathe* at her. She finally gulped some air into her lungs and fought to steady herself.

Fortunately, her sister-in-law didn't sense the undercurrents, or if she did, she ignored them. "You do want to come with us to see her, don't you?" Meredith asked. "I can pick you up with the helicopter and then fly us to Ft. Worth on the ranch's jet. We'll only be gone a couple of days at the most."

Abby's body was calmer, her breathing regulated. She wanted very much to see her new niece, but…

"Don't worry about Gray, if that's what's stopping you," Cinco cut in.

Gray wished that Cinco and Meredith would go away. He wanted to talk to Abby. Wanted to find out how she was doing and what she was feeling. He'd sensed her pain and needed to do something or say something to help. But Cinco had turned to address him, so he remained still.

"I have some news in that regard, too," Cinco said, smiling. "It looks like maybe we've come up with a good reason why someone would want to see you hurt, Parker. Actually, it seems incredible, but I guess since you didn't hire an attorney to protect your interests when your mother died, there would be no way for a nonlawyer like yourself to understand this."

"What?" Gray asked, with renewed interest.

"Your mother left you something besides the mustangs," Cinco told him. "As you might know, her will transferred everything she had kept separately from Joe Skaggs into an irrevocable trust for you…to be kept for your benefit until you turn thirty and can inherit it outright."

"Yes, I do know that. I won't be thirty for a couple of years yet, though," Gray replied. "What does that have to do with what my mother left me?"

Cinco's eyes became serious. His expression was sober and daunting. "Well, it seems that a few years ago, Joe Skaggs let himself get into big financial trouble. He owed everybody in the state and was on the verge of losing his ranch. Your mother agreed to bail him out of his trouble by using some of the proceeds of the mustang sales and stud fees to pay down his debt.''

Gray's heart constricted. Why hadn't his mother ever called him and told him what was going on? He would've come home to help them out.

''But your mother was a real smart businesswoman, Gray,'' Cinco continued. ''With every penny she paid against Joe's loans, she acquired a proportional ownership of Skaggs Ranch in her separate name. Right before she died the part she owned had grown past the fifty percent mark.''

Cinco's eyes crinkled into a sly smile. ''When you turn thirty, you'll have the majority control of the Skaggs Ranch. Joe only has a forty-nine percent share. You could kick him off his own land if you had a mind to.''

Gray was stunned and speechless. But his brain quickly started putting pieces together. There were some long-term ramifications of this that he had yet to come to terms with, but for now he could feel the anger climbing up his spine.

''So, you think Joe Skaggs has been trying to kill me? To try to get control of his land back?'' Gray gritted his teeth and jerked up from the table. ''My stepfather was the one who hurt Abby?''

Cinco shook his head and stood, too. ''Whoa. Unfortunately, that theory doesn't make sense. I wish it was that easy. But if you die, your property, including the trust, would not go back to Joe Skaggs. After all, I doubt that you've got a will leaving your worldly possessions to your stepfather, do you?''

Gray shook his head and jammed his hands into his pockets.

''No, I didn't think so. It would either go to your next of kin...like your grandfather or maybe to Abby if you two were married. Or if neither one of those was available, it would go to the State of Texas.'' Cinco moved next to him and placed a hand on his shoulder. ''I think Joe is smart enough to know he'd be better off taking his chances with you than with the state.''

''Then who's been doing this?'' Gray muttered.

''Well, my money's on one of the boys,'' Cinco said with a smile. ''Neither one of them is smart enough to understand wills and trusts. But both of them are devious enough to think they could gain something by killing you off.''

''Is the sheriff going to arrest them both?'' Abby asked.

''No, honey,'' Cinco told her. ''He doesn't have enough evidence yet. But he's got a man following both of them day and night. There won't be any surprise attacks from now on. I'll bet that before too long one of them cracks, anyhow.''

Cinco turned back to Gray. ''I think you'd better stay out here and away from the Skaggs Ranch until the sheriff has someone in custody, though. I don't believe you're in any real danger anymore. You can relax.''

Cinco then grabbed up Abby with one huge arm and grinned at Gray. ''So tell my little sister here that she can take a couple of days off from being your bodyguard and is free to go visit Cal's baby, will you?''

While Abby had been away, Gray had found himself hungry for a glimpse of her. She'd only been gone for thirty-six hours, but it had seemed like a lifetime without her smile.

Cinco and Meredith had brought a ton of supplies with them, so Gray managed to keep himself busy during that time. They'd delivered foodstuffs, a portable washing machine and more building supplies. A bathtub and a new cooking stove were the most notable things.

And...of course...there was the big king-size bed and mattress. Maybe it had been when he'd placed that bed inside the cabin that this desperate craving to be with Abby had begun to take over his whole being.

She'd arrived back at the cabin only a few short minutes ago, looking fantastic. Rested, happy and eager to tell him all about her new niece.

If he'd stopped to really think about it, he'd have wondered why it seemed that his heart had only restarted the minute Abby came into view. But he didn't want to think too much at the moment. He just wanted to enjoy listening to her and watching her as she immediately pitched in to help him with his work.

She was dressed in her typical jeans and plaid work shirt and looked ready to get her hands dirty. Now that he had his helper back to assist him, the work would go much faster. That is if he could keep his own hands to himself.

"You did so much while I was gone," she said as she handed him a wrench. "The place is really shaping up."

The sun was drenching them both in a hot, liquid glare. But Abby seemed to soak it up. She watched him work on the last of the pipes that would bring enough water into the house to run the washing machine and to take a real bath.

Without Gray having to ask, Abby had recognized his need for the wrench and handed it to him. She'd moved toward it even before he'd thought of it himself. They made a wonderful working team, he mused in silence. In fact, they were as well matched as the male and female flanges on the pipes he'd just fitted together.

The blinding truth hit him instantly. He knew that he loved her in one flashing bit of unconscious insight. Could it really be as simple and as complicated as that?

Now that he knew about his love, what he should *do* with that knowledge left him utterly dumbfounded. He couldn't marry her. But even at the risk of making the ancient ones angry with him, he knew he could never leave her, either.

"Gray?" She said his name, and the music in her voice turned him into a panting puppy. "Did you get much work done on the cabin's interior while I was gone?"

The question took him by surprise, but he recovered quickly enough. "Uh, yes, quite a bit. Would you like to come inside and see it?" he asked her warily.

She nodded. "I want to tell you what Cinco said to me while we were on the way to Ft. Worth, too. He made me so mad. I was absolutely furious…until Meredith made me think about it a little more and I realized he was right."

Gray set his tools aside and wiped his hands on a rag. "You want to tell me about it inside? The refrigerator is working now. We can have a cold drink and talk." He hesitated a second. "That is, if you think you can bear to be inside the cabin that long."

"I want to try," she said. "It's important that I try."

Gray opened the door and ushered her out of the dripping heat and into the cool shade of the wood- and rock-walled cabin. She slowed to a stop a few feet inside the door.

He stepped behind her and placed his hands on her shoulders, steadying her. "You doing okay?" he whispered.

She didn't turn or step ahead, but placed one of her

hands over one of his as if to capture his calm. "Yes," she told him in a shaky voice. "Oh, Gray, you've done a great job. It looks the way I always pictured it would look."

"There's a lot more work to do, but I think it's livable now, at any rate." He heard a rumble from outdoors and smelled the pungent odor of rain moving in.

She still didn't move away, only leaned back against his chest and sighed. "Cinco called me his 'little missy' one time too many while we were gone, and I screamed at him to start treating me like an adult. He said I'd never be grown-up until I learned how to get over my mother's disappearance and could stay inside her cabin and face it."

Gray wished he could see Abby's eyes so he could decide how best to handle this—what to say to make her feel better. But he sensed she needed the warmth and strength of his embrace more at this moment, so he wrapped his arms around her shoulders, trapping her back next to his heart.

"I was mad. I didn't want to hear that from him," she confessed. "But Meredith made me see that I could cherish my mother's memory, yet still come to terms with the fact that she isn't coming back. I need…and want…to build my own life."

He leaned his cheek down on the top of her head and tightened his grip. "Don't be so hard on yourself. All it takes is a little work and a little time." Gray heard the patter of rain against the roof and was glad he'd thrown a tarp over his tools. "I'll stand with you, Abby. I'll be right here if you need to lean on me."

She twisted around to face him then, but stayed within his arms. "I have something else in mind besides leaning,'' she grinned. ''I've brought some things I want to show you.''

A crack of thunder rumbled through the cabin, but more important, a deep sensual seduction shone in her gaze.

Eleven

Abby stood on tiptoe, dragged Gray down by the neck and placed a soft kiss against his lips. He heard the blood rushing to his head…roaring…blocking out the thunder.

He tried to take a breath, but she'd invaded his system. Not only weren't his lungs functioning, but his brain had ceased to work, as well. Honor, duty, promises…all were lost to him. Replaced by the one single desire—Abby.

His mouth crushed down on hers, hot, heavy and demanding. The beat of his heart pounded in his ears until he didn't know whether the constant drumming was coming from his pulse or a furious storm outside.

She had a basic taste, like everything good and fresh about the damp earth after the rain. He wanted all of it. All of the essence of Abby.

He crammed his thigh between her legs and lifted her up onto the tabletop. Abby went wild. And Gray suddenly felt as if they were at war, ripping and tearing as if each other's clothes, fighting for the feel of skin against skin. In the back of his mind he vaguely remembered her saying something about showing him something, but in this frenzy all he wanted was to have her naked beside him.

Finally, when they were free of their clothing, he fed on her smell and on her taste. He nipped the skin above the soft swell of her naked breast, while she made a greedy little sound and nibbled on his bare shoulder in return.

She leaned backward to lie on the table, so he smoothed his hands over her soft, creamy skin, finding all the sensitive places. Replacing his fingers with his mouth, he licked, sucked, cherished her. His control was destroyed.

She flexed her muscles, arched against him. Her strength was more than erotic. He ran his hand over the corded muscles in her thighs, and she shuddered. Suddenly he wanted her weakness as well as her strength. He wanted everything.

The shock of their violent intimacy exploded the civilized being he was and left a pulsating, aroused beast in his place. Somehow the primitive savage inside him had managed to escape.

Now. He had to be inside her—now. He flipped her over, facedown on the table, and she braced her feet on the floor. He used one hand to hold her still as he moved his hands over her back and down across her buttocks.

Abby moaned and arched her hips toward him. He spread her thighs, then slid a hand underneath her and placed it low on her belly. Lifting her hips even higher, he slowly fitted himself into her waiting core. He was unbearably aroused and growing thicker as all the blood rushed to his groin.

She tipped her pelvis, drawing him deeper, and he lost whatever control was left. He rammed himself hard against her, and she gasped, rocking and undulating against him. Nothing mattered now but the mewling little sounds of pleasure she made as he thrust faster.

He felt her going over the edge. Felt the mating and the branding as his own response overpowered him. When the climax winged through them both like an arrow, it pinned his soul to hers for eternity—while his own essence spilled into her with a triumphant rush.

A winded moment later Gray was shaking, but he lifted her up in his arms, kissing every inch of her within reach. He carried her into the bedroom and collapsed with her onto the bed.

She landed, splayed out across his chest. He loved the feel of her there. Running his hand up and down her spine, he knew when her trembling stopped and she went limp, relaxing against him.

"I love you," he murmured, kissing her temple.

Abby stilled, stopped breathing. All he could feel was the thudding of her heart, keeping time with his.

"Abby. Did you hear me? I love you."

She rolled away from him and sat up. Her eyes were clouded over, as suddenly dark and stormy as the thundershower outside had been.

"I heard you," she said in a cold tone. "What do you mean by that?"

He was struck with an icy fear. "I mean, I want to be with you forever. I want to take care of you. I want you to take care of me. It means I need you."

"Are you asking me to marry you?"

He sat up, reached for her, but she backed away. "I haven't thought that far ahead," he admitted. "I just know that wherever I go, I want you beside me. I'm just not sure how that's going to happen yet."

She stood, turned and went into the front room. He followed her as she stooped to pick up her clothes.

Shivers of doubt ran down his spine and he braced himself. "Abby, sweetheart. You haven't said anything. Do you love me?"

She shook her head, but it seemed to be more in frustration than an actual answer. "I...don't know how I feel. I know I want to be with you, too, but...but I..." She let her words trail off as she climbed into her jeans.

The hurt and the pride clutched at his chest. "You just don't love me enough to commit to leaving the Gentry Ranch when I follow the mustangs, is that it?"

Abby hung her head, devastated by her own hesitation. She was pretty sure that leaving the Gentry was not the problem. But what was the matter with her, anyway? She just hadn't had a chance to really think about loving Gray. Oh, she'd thought plenty about *making* love with him, but not about being *in love.* No, that was totally another question.

From somewhere outside, she could hear the rain as it softly hit the hard-packed ground. She felt the drizzle begin in her heart, as well.

This was too much to think about right now. Love? Need? She knew she wanted him...wanted to stay beside him. But right now all she felt was a numbing fear. The shivers seemed to start deep down in her gut, stalking up her muscles until her whole body was cold and shaking.

She hugged her arms tightly around her chest, hoping to stem the shakes. Wouldn't it be better if Gray put his arms around her to give her his strength and warmth the way he had so often in the past?

Abby looked up and found that Gray had dressed and was throwing a few things into one of his packs. "What are you doing?" she asked tentatively.

"I'm going back to Skaggs Ranch. I've been neglecting the mustangs...and I need to check on my grandfather and...do a few other chores, too."

Her panic turned to terror. "You're leaving? But...but what about the stalker? Even if we knew for sure it was one of your brothers, he might still try to sneak up on you."

Gray narrowed his eyes at her, then shrugged a shoulder. "You'll be fine. If you're frightened, just stay away from Skaggs Ranch and call your brother, he'll protect you." He set his jaw and lifted the pack. "You don't have to worry about watching my back anymore. I can take care of myself. Our deal and the fake engagement is off."

She opened her mouth to speak, but no words came out, so she cleared her throat and tried again. "But you said you owed me your life. You said you'd always protect me," she whispered in a hoarse rasp.

Gray headed for the cabin door, stopped, but didn't turn to face her. "As long as you're on the Gentry Ranch, your brother can do a better job of protecting you than I can. If you really need me...some day in the future...just give me a call. I'll be around." He stomped out the door without ever looking back.

And then he was really gone. Abby crumpled to the floor and wept bitter, selfish tears. She should've been prepared for something like this. People who said they loved you always left you behind. What else could she have expected?

Gray sat cross-legged and perfectly still on the pallet of hides in his lodge, trying to ignore both his leg cramps and the hunger pains. For four days now, he'd been here, fasting and praying to the ancients for guidance. And still there were no answers. There was nothing but his own confused thoughts to haunt him.

After he'd ridden away from Abby's cabin, over a week ago now, he'd checked on both the mustangs and his grandfather. All was well. He hadn't heard from Abby since then, but he couldn't get her out of his mind.

He absently rubbed his palm across his heart.

When he'd first come back onto Skaggs property, he'd made a point of trying to find his stepfather. But Joe Skaggs had mysteriously disappeared.

Gray hadn't run into Milan or Harold, either, but he reluctantly admitted that he hadn't really tried to search them out. If one of those two imbeciles was responsible for hurting Abby, he was half-afraid of what he might do to them.

No. After due consideration, Gray thought it would be the smartest choice if he let the sheriff handle the Skaggs boys. What Gray needed to do most of all was to plead for guidance with a new vision quest. His heart and his head were aching and raw. He'd made promises, both to the elders and to Abby. His honor demanded that he keep them both.

He knew it was his duty to take the mustangs back to the ancient hunting grounds. Just like he knew his future bride must be determined by the *nemene*. And he remembered his promise to protect Abby always…but then, she didn't need his protection.

A searing new thought branded his soul: *She doesn't need me…for anything.* She's strong and rich and capable of taking care of herself.

Gray swiveled to stoke the flames in the cookstove. He wanted it hotter—steamier—in here. He'd sweat out his confusion, if nothing else was working. He wanted a rededication to his original principles. If he meant nothing to Abby Gentry, then he would find his soul, back with the mustangs and his people.

While splashing a little spray of water onto the fire, Gray once again heard the drumming of the rain on the lodge's roof. The spring rains hadn't let up since the day he'd left the Gentry Ranch. A constant drizzle, complete with misty ground fog and the smell of damp leather, had become like an old friend.

A backlash of steam from the fire filled his nostrils with the smell of mesquite and herbs. His eyes teared from the smoke, and he blinked to clear them.

You seek our guidance, Gray Wolf Parker?

Through the wisps of a shadowy cloud, Gray saw Pia, the Great Mother of all the people, standing before him.

"Yes, wise one," he whispered. "I am lost. I cannot find my way."

It is always wisest to follow your heart, my son.

"But my heart leads me to one who is not of our blood. She cannot be the choice of the elders for my bride."

The one who is chosen carries your ancestors' seed. Look deeper, Gray Wolf Parker. Look into the foggy shrouds of time to find your answers. Your heart has not lied to you.

Gray felt a sudden chill and huddled against it. Through the opaque vapor, he saw Pia reaching out to him. The blurry shadows now bore an edgy feel of danger.

Your chosen one searches for you...but the two-headed snake stands between.

He wondered what the elder was trying to say. He had so many more questions, so much more confusion. What about the mustangs? What about... He had the feeling this vision was coming to an end.

"I don't understand," he cried. "Please tell me..."

Go now, my son. Follow your heart. You are needed.

Abby hunkered down farther into her rain slicker. The drizzle had become more of a steady stream, and she cussed lightly under her breath as she fought to reshoe her gelding.

Of all the times for her horse to pick up a rock, this might be the worst. Oh, it wasn't that she couldn't take care of it herself, all the ranch hands on the Gentry Ranch did their own shoeing. But right this minute all Abby wanted to do was to find Gray.

Except...maybe she'd like to be off this muddy prairie and out of the rain.

She was searching for Gray because she had so much to tell him—and the danged man still didn't have a cell phone so she could call him. She sighed, figuring it was probably better to say what she had to say in person, anyway.

Abby had learned so much over the past week, about who she really was and what she really wanted. There were some hard-fought battles she'd waged inside herself, but the skirmishes were over and she knew her heart. She could only pray that Gray still cared enough to hear her out—that she hadn't destroyed everything when she'd let him walk away.

A slight rustle in the bushes to her right made Abby lift her head to see what was there. She didn't see much because the gigantic drops of Texas sunshine came pouring off the brim of her work hat and into her eyes as she'd raised her chin.

She shrugged it off, figuring the noise might be one of the mustangs trying to find shelter from the storm. Looking for Gray, she'd stopped by the Skaggses' main house, but she hadn't found anyone there—not even a ranch hand she could ask. But she'd known where else to look. Gray had to be either at his lodge or out here tending to his herd.

She bent down to finish her task so she could be on her way when another noise, this time the sound of a horse's gallop, made her rise up again. What she saw absolutely took her breath away.

Gray rode toward her on the back of his sleek, black mustang. Naked to the waist, he wore simple leggings, moccasins and a soft leather breechcloth. His slick black hair hung almost to his broad shoulders. A necklace, made from some kind of cloth pouch and two hawk's feathers, hung around his neck. With the rain, gliding wet and sensuously over his bronzed chest, Abby thought the man was too good to be true. Perhaps she'd wanted to see him so badly that this was really a dream.

The dream pulled his horse up beside her, slid off its back and grabbed her by the shoulders. "Abby, why are you on Skaggs land? You could be in danger here."

Gray was really there, really touching her. "I've come to tell you some things…ask you…some things."

He stood close enough that she could feel the steam rising off his sweaty chest and warming her soul. She was desperate for the feel of his arms around her but knew she had to wait. She just hoped it wouldn't be for long.

"Can we move to somewhere safer…and drier…first?" he asked solemnly.

She searched his dear face for her answers, but all she found were the beloved angles of his jaw and a pointed stare. "No, I have to tell you…" she breathed. "I love you, Gray. I guess I've always loved you. I just couldn't admit it to myself before."

"You've decided *now* you love me?" he demanded dryly.

The first stabbing arrow of doubt hit her then. It couldn't be too late. She wouldn't let it be too late.

"Please," she begged. "Let me finish. I didn't know I could love anyone. When my mother disappeared, I thought everyone I ever let myself love would eventually leave me, too. I was scared...mad. I hid away inside my little girl's skin and let the world go on around me. If I didn't grow up, I didn't have to face all the pain."

"What's changed?" Gray asked warily.

She swallowed back the sob that was about to choke her. "After I spent a few days alone in Mother's cabin, searching my heart, I finally forgave her for leaving me. I'm not angry about her disappearance anymore." Abby looked into the eyes of the man she loved. "I want to come outside into the world and...let myself need love. I need you, Gray. I need your love."

He set his jaw, turned his chin to stare into the brush. This just couldn't be so.

"Gray, I beg you. Don't turn away from me. I want to go wherever you go. I'll follow you to the ends of the earth, if that's where the mustangs take you." She was sobbing openly now, her tears mingling with the drops of rain against her cheeks.

She reached up to throw her arms around his neck, trying to pull him close so at least his body might remember the feel of hers.

"Abby," he shouted gruffly. As he pushed at her roughly, she fell away from him. "Get back! Watch out!"

The next few seconds were a blur of sound and fury. Gray shoved her body in between his and the horse's, while from somewhere off in the distance she heard shouts...anger...shots being fired. With a sudden crack of what she thought must be thunder, a sharp pain drove into her upper arm. But it felt like only a minor irritation compared to the pain in her heart.

Gray had palmed his knife long before the first shot was fired. He started for the brush, determined to finish this right now. Never again would they be stalked this way.

A bullet ripped past his ear as he bent to rush the shooter. Before he could take one more step, a second shot, this one from a distance, rang out. He heard a muffled moan, from ahead and behind him, then more shots and some shouting in the distance. Then the shooting stopped. All was quiet.

"Gray!" The pain he heard in Abby's voice cleared the red haze of anger from his brain and he turned back to her.

What he saw made his heart lurch. She was kneeling in the mud while blood streamed out of her shoulder, mixing with the rain and cascading down her body in sheets that seemed almost pink.

He knew she must be in pain, but still she held both arms out to him in a pleading gesture. "Wait, Gray. Wait for me. Don't leave me," she cried.

"Oh, Great Spirit! Abby, you've been shot." He dropped his knife into the mud and went to her.

He bent on one knee before her and gently slid his arm around her waist to steady her. He saw that her wound was not life threatening, but still it nearly killed him to see her in pain once again. At least the blood flow had dwindled to a slow ooze. He silently gave thanks.

"Abby, my Abby." He shook his head and swiped at the rain that was blurring his vision. "I'll never leave you again, my love. Never. It's all my fault you've been hurt. I let my pride stand in the way of my duty."

"Duty?" she whimpered. "Is that all you feel toward me?"

He shook his head in wonder at her innocent appeal. "Sometimes I get so mad at you I could just strangle you. Other times…I'm blinded by the passionate siren you can be," he told her softly. "But always…always…I love you with every fiber, every breath in me."

He hesitated in order to fight for air and calm. "I'm afraid you will never be rid of me now, dear heart. You might as well marry me and get used to having me around."

"Marry you?" she asked in a shaky voice. "But I thought the tribe—the elders…"

"It doesn't matter, love. Nothing matters but you. Shush…hush now. I need to wrap your arm and stop—"

From behind him, Gray heard someone moving toward them from the brush. He eyed Abby's rifle, still in its spot, hanging on her saddle. Just as he was about to push off for the gun, he heard someone calling his name.

"Mr. Parker? Miss Gentry? Are y'all okay?" A sheriff's deputy whom Gray had met before came from around a tangle of mesquite. "There you two are." The man pointed his rifle barrel at the ground and put a hand on his hip.

"Miss Gentry's arm has been grazed, Deputy." Gray stood to take the first-aid kit from Abby's pack. "She's in no immediate danger, but she'll need to see a doctor."

He dug into the kit, determined to find the gauze and antiseptic, despite the fact that his hands were still shaking. "What's happening out in the bush?" Gray asked the deputy.

The sheriff's man narrowed his eyes at Abby's wound and scratched his chin. "Well, dang," he said with a shake of his head. "I'd sure hoped that one shot ol'

Milan managed to pull off had gone wild. I'm mighty grateful it weren't worse'n that, ma'am."

"Milan?" Abby asked. "So it was Milan who's been after Gray?"

The deputy shrugged a shoulder. "Seems both them Skaggs boys have been plotting to do away with their stepbrother, ma'am." He moved closer to stare at her arm. "I'm sure sorry about this, Miss Gentry. You going to be all right?"

"I'll be fine. It's just a scratch." She looked up at Gray as he bent down again, this time with the antiseptic and bandages in his hand. "I assume that you've captured Milan Skaggs, Deputy. What about Harold?"

"Couldn't manage to take ol' Milan...alive, ma'am. I followed him out here while he tracked you from the Skaggs' main house," the deputy told her. "The sheriff said I wasn't to make a move until Milan made some threatening gesture toward y'all. I kinda lost sight of him for a second, what with all the downpour, and before I knew it he'd gotten a shot off.

"I dropped him where he stood." The deputy shuffled his feet and hung his head. "I sure wish I'd been a minute faster. For your sake, ma'am."

Abby gasped as Gray spread the antiseptic ointment over her wound, and he had to grit his teeth to finish the job. He couldn't bear that she was hurting, but he was sure glad the bleeding had stopped and it looked like she'd be fine.

"What about Harold?" he asked the deputy.

"One of the other men has been following Harold, Mr. Parker. Looks like that Skaggs boy was following his brother while he tracked you. When the first shots were fired, Harold raised his rifle to take aim on you, one last time.

"Our man drew down on him, but in the confusion,

Harold managed to get away.'' The deputy straightened up, looked as if he was ready to move on. ''If you're sure you're okay here, I need to join the rest of the sheriff's men. It won't be more than a few hours afore we catch up to ol' Harold. He's got no place to hide.'' The deputy took his leave and disappeared back into the brush the way he came.

Gray finished bandaging Abby's arm. ''Are you going to make a fuss when I call in the paramedics' helicopter to take you to the hospital?'' he chuckled.

She smiled back at him. ''Nope. Especially not since my cell phone has gone dead again.''

''Ah. I see that you really do need me. At least to remind you to plug your phone in,'' he teased. ''So. Are you going to marry me?''

Abby grinned up at him, but still had a hesitant look in her eyes. ''What about your people?''

By way of a partial answer, Gray caressed her cheek and then lightly kissed her lips. ''By any chance, chosen one, do you have a little Indian blood in your background?''

''As a matter of fact, I do.'' She beamed. ''On my mother's side.

Epilogue

The sun shone brightly down on Abby's bare head. Meanwhile, a light spring breeze tousled the ends of her hair and swirled the silken folds of her dress around her ankles as she turned to find her brand-new husband in the crowd.

She spotted Gray with no trouble. He was standing, lost in deep conversation with the sheriff and Jake Gomez. But as she admired how grand he looked in his buckskin suit and with his hair pulled back and tied in a leather thong, he seemed to sense her need. He lifted his head, found her eyes immediately and smiled at her.

It had only been a week since the sheriff had captured Harold and they'd buried Milan. She and Gray might've waited a little longer to take their wedding vows, but she couldn't really think of a good reason why.

Abby looked around at the friends and family who had gathered here at her mother's cabin to celebrate her marriage. Gray's grandfather had come from Oklahoma and looked quite distinguished in his traditional tribal garb. Meredith had flown up in the jet and brought him back, along with Abby's brother Cal and Cal's new wife and baby.

All the people she loved were here. A little wistful tug at her heart reminded her that her parents were not among the guests today. But she only smiled through the ache, knowing they were here in spirit.

Even Joe Skaggs had come to their ceremony, but Jake had had to bring him out in a wheelchair. It seemed that Joe was dying of cancer—something both of Gray's stepbrothers had known, though no one else had guessed.

When he'd found himself about to die, Joe apparently had been attacked by a sudden remorse for the way he'd treated Gray and his mother and had changed his will, leaving the balance of the Skaggs ranch to Gray. When Harold and Milan found out, they'd decided to try to get rid of Gray by making it look like an accident.

But Joe had been taken to the hospital just as Gray had returned to Skaggs Ranch. Desperate to kill Gray before their father died and they lost their last chance to inherit, the boys had gone after their stepbrother in earnest.

Abby was glad that Gray had invited Joe Skaggs to the wedding. The man was dying, with one son who'd died before him and one son in prison for good. Gray seemed to be coming to terms with his long-term dislike for his stepfather.

She was also very glad when she looked up and saw the other half of her soul, making his way through the crowd toward her. With every step closer Gray took, her heart and her body became heated with the warmth of her love for him.

He swung her close and whispered in her ear. "When can we make all these folks go home, love? I want to lie with my new wife. And I can't wait much longer for your touch or the feel of your skin rubbing across my skin, either."

She giggled as he nuzzled her neck, but she was in full agreement with his sentiments. They'd planned to spend several days out here in her mother's cabin for their honeymoon before they set out on a search for the mustangs' ancient grounds and a new place to call home. And she had at least several days' worth of unused lingerie that she could scarcely wait to try on for him during that time.

"If you'll find a way to speed our family on their way," she murmured in his ear, "I have a few surprises I'd like to show you."

He pulled back to look at her, and a grin creased his features. "That sounds like a plan to me, sweetheart." A twinkle, more devilish than sensual, shone in his eyes. "I have a little surprise for you, too."

"What is it, Gray? Tell me now," she softly demanded.

"You know I can't deny you anything," he sighed against her hair. "Jake has been telling me about how all the land around here used to be full of buffalo, before the white settlers arrived. I guess the Gentry and the Skaggs ranches were right in the path of their migrations."

She didn't know where this was going but she nodded. "Yes that's right. I remember the stories now. The Comanche used to hunt all through these parts."

The meaning of his words hit her at the same moment

he opened his mouth to finish his tale. "I asked Grandfather about it. He told me that the legends of the ancient hunting grounds spoke of wild ponies and herds of buffalo as far south as Mexico and as far west as the Rocky Mountains." Gray smiled down on her. "That means the mustangs are already home, Abby."

Tears sprang into her eyes, blurring the sight of the dear face of the man she knew she'd love forever. "Then..." she murmured past the frog in her throat. "We don't have to leave? We can live in Mother's little cabin and stay on Gentry Ranch for good?"

"Abby Gentry Parker, I will go wherever you want to go until our life's vision is ended. You are my soul...my chosen one. Name the place, and there I will build my life with you."

He scooped her up in his arms and rained kisses down on her tear-streaked face. "From this day forward. Wherever in the world you happen to find yourself at home...will be my home, too."

* * * * *

COMING NEXT MONTH

#1519 SCENES OF PASSION—Suzanne Brockmann
Maggie Stanton knew something was missing from her picture-perfect life, and when she ran into her high school buddy Michael Stone, she knew just what it was. The former bad boy had grown into a charismatic man who was everything Maggie had ever dreamed of. But if they were to have a future together, Maggie would have to learn to trust him.

#1520 CINDERELLA'S MILLIONAIRE—Katherine Garbera
Dynasties: The Barones
Love was the last thing on widower Joseph Barone's mind…until he was roped into escorting pastry chef Holly Fitzgerald to a media interview. The brooding millionaire had built an impenetrable wall around his heart, but delectable Holly was pure temptation. He needed her—in his bed and in his life—but was he ready to risk his heart again?

#1521 IN BED WITH THE ENEMY—Kathie DeNosky
Lone Star Country Club
ATF agent Cole Yardley didn't believe women belonged in the field, fighting crime, but then a gun-smuggling investigation brought him and FBI agent Elise Campbell together. Though he'd intended to ignore Elise, Cole soon found himself surrendering to the insatiable hunger she stirred in him.…

#1522 EXPECTING THE COWBOY'S BABY—Charlene Sands
An old flame came roaring back to life when Cassie Munroe went home for her brother's wedding and ran into Jake Griffin, her high school ex. The boy who'd broken her heart was gone, and in his place was one sinfully sexy man. They wound up sharing an unforgettable night of passion that would change Cassie's life forever, for now she was pregnant with Jake's baby!

#1523 CHEROKEE DAD—Sheri WhiteFeather
Desperate to keep her nephew safe, Heather Richmond turned to Michael Elk, the man she'd left behind eighteen months ago. Michael still touched her soul in a way no other man ever had, and she couldn't resist the seductive promises in his eyes. She only hoped he would forgive her once he discovered her secret.…

#1524 THE GENTRYS: CAL—Linda Conrad
When Cal Gentry went home to his family ranch to recover from the accident that killed his wife, he found Isabella de la Cruz on his doorstep. The mysterious beauty needed protecting…and soon found a sense of security in Cal's arms. Then, as things heated up between them, Cal vowed to convince Isabella to accept not only his protection, but his heart, as well.

SDCNM0603